CHANGELING

A STEAMPUNK ROMANCE

JODI KENDRICK

SOULGATE PUBLISHING

Copyright © 2023 by Jodi Kendrick

Book Cover by Dar Albert, Wicked Smart Designs

Editing by Kim Ross

Published by SoulGate Publishing

https://soulgate.org

Jodi Kendrick

Romance. Adventure. Passion.

Dragon Island
Dragon Heat

Enchanted Ardor
Wish

EveL Worlds : FUCN'A
Tough Nut
Diamond in the Ruff
Honeyed Nut
Gorilla in the Hiss
FUCN'A Collection One
Pedigree Collection

Finely Aged
Dragon Steel

Global Paranormal Security Agency
Awakened
Surfacing
Polestar
Aquatic Investigations
Prowler

The Kindred Chronicles
Healer
Mercenary

The Soaring Dragon Chronicles
Return Flight
Changeling

Love and Adventure aboard the luxury airship
The Soaring Dragon.

CHAPTER ONE

LIN MEI LAU ADMIRED the elegant lines of the *Soaring Dragon* as it floated toward its mooring above Victoria Harbour on Hong Kong Island.

The balloon gleamed and the gondola glinted in the sunlight, high above the sparkling water.

She sighed, soaking up the sight of the golden luxury airship.

Some day.

She was bound for the harbor front on an errand for her mother, from her mountain village home on the mainland side of the Hong Kong region. She rested on the box of rice wine she would sell at her spot by the Victoria Hotel. Businessmen from all over the world bought her mother's wine.

It was 'Hong Kong's best', she told them.

The proof of their agreement would weigh her hidden pocket with their coin all the way home.

Shielding her eyes with her hand, she checked the angle of the sun, returning her gaze to the distant airship.

Her brother, Andrew Siu Lung Lau, had taken on the post of Chief of Security aboard the Soaring Dragon a little over a year ago, and he was coming home for an extended stay.

The unloading of passengers and cargo would begin soon.

Time to go, Lin Mei.

Standing, she lifted the crate, balanced it on her head, and resumed her journey with a lighter step.

Humming to herself, she recalled the few stories Andrew had recounted during his quick stops home while the ship was at port.

Who would have guessed an airship could be so full of adventure?

Someday I'm going to work aboard the Soaring Dragon, too.

She laughed.

Andrew would hate the idea.

The dirt path quickly turned to packed earth roads as her imagination soared with the possibilities that the airship offered.

The streets were already bustling when she set her crate of wine on the ground before the grand hotel. The sun was a little higher than it should have been for her arrival, so she quickly got to work.

An hour later, her crate was empty and her pocket full. She surreptitiously tucked the linen purse so that it dropped inside her clothing, out of view—and reach—of the sticky fingers of wharf thieves.

Taking up the crate, she crossed the road, mindful of horses and rickshaws, to the food hawker's stall at the edge of the market.

The air by the waterfront differed from the mountain air she was used to.

Heavier, saltier. Smelly.

Soon her crate held fresh fruit and steamed buns for her three energetic younger siblings. Navigating the crush of people, she made her way to the ferry depot to wait for Andrew and Adelina.

Boosting herself up onto canvas-covered cargo, she settled comfortably and unwrapped one of the tasty buns for herself.

Well-to-do businessmen wandered by in conversation, discussing the latest economic developments, while foreigners strolled past in varying degrees of wonder of all that Hong Kong had to offer.

They all wore their dark suits with three-quarter length suit jackets, top hats, and carried walking sticks or umbrellas with fancy polished handles.

As part of the British Empire, it was a thriving hub of trade goods and people.

Lin Mei eavesdropped on anyone within earshot. She'd picked up a few languages, having spent so much time interacting with the harbor front clientele. The harbor was a miniature of the greater world beyond the little island and its surrounding territory.

All the world, right here, in Hong Kong.

Her eyes drifted back to the moored airship at the island-side dock, just a short ferry ride across the glittering expanse of Victoria Harbour.

Nibbling at her aromatic sweet bun, she engaged in her favorite daydream.

Could I successfully stow away if I wanted to?

She amused herself, plotting the string of events required to do it.

I'd rather be there legitimately.

Like Andrew.

It had been a favor to his superior officer at the Constabulary. The police chief's famous father-in-law, Toussaint Kaisin, had needed a trusted personal guard during his travels back to Europe. He'd insisted that Andrew was the right man for the job, making it difficult for him to refuse. The position became permanent after Andrew and Adelina reunited during that trip.

I'll ask him this *time*.

He'd be home long enough that she had time to wear him down.

Worrying her lip, Lin Mei considered her options.

Literate, but not formally educated. Hard working. And at twenty-two, she *should* have been married with children of her own by now.

Lin Mei wasn't interested in making a match, no matter how suitable her mother thought the young men working in the market or surrounding farms were. Lin Mei had already ruled out fishermen. As much as she loved eating fish, she'd rather not smell like them for the rest of her life.

The weight of the purse tied to her waist seemed to grow as she thought of the responsibilities she was expected to fulfill.

From across the harbor, the ferry's stack spewed forth its cloud as it pulled away from its dock, turning toward her.

Her worries puffed away like the ferry smoke, and she smiled.

Andrew was home.

PROFESSOR JOSEPH KAISIN FINISHED reviewing the inventory with a nod, then handed the list back to the stevedore foreman. They loaded the furniture and larger pieces of equipment aboard a sea-going ship. The rest would accompany him aboard the Soaring Dragon.

His father's household. A lifetime of work, collections, and mementos. The more precious items would travel with him.

"Joe!"

He turned to see his old school friend, Andrew Lau, approaching him along the pier, accompanied by a striking auburn-haired beauty.

"Andrew! Adelina! I wondered if I'd see you here. My father has been raving about you in his letters." He smiled and kissed the back of Adelina's gloved hand, noting her extended belly. "I wanted to thank you both for your service in keeping my father and his work safe during his voyage to Europe."

"How is Mr. Kaisin?" she asked.

"His health has turned." Joe waved a hand toward the crates stacked on the wharf next to them. "I've finally convinced him to remain in London with me now that I'm seriously thinking of taking a post at the university there. I'll tell you, he is not happy about it, but I think it's for the best."

"Chief Clayton has kept us up to date on the matter of the break-ins to your father's Hong Kong house. The events here could be connected to what happened on the Soaring Dragon. I'm sure the Chief will be sorry to lose Mr. Kaisin's companionship," Andrew said.

Joe nodded. "He was equally sorry to see you leave the constabulary as a result of my father's adventures. Should we go somewhere for tea, Adelina?" Joe offered as her gloved hand swept her extended belly.

She was about to answer when a young woman appeared, calling Andrew's Chinese name.

"Lin Mei!" Andrew smiled and responded in the local dialect.

A small woman with bright eyes, a lovely smile, and delicate features framed by wisps of black hair escaping the knot at her nape approached and set her crate down.

Breathtaking.

Adelina's smile broadened upon seeing the young woman. "Andrew's sister," she said to Joe.

The siblings' exchange continued on another moment, ending with a warm embrace before they turned to the present company. Andrew first introduced Adelina to his sister, then Joe, who greeted her politely.

Her smile was wide, and her eyes sparkled as she nodded to them. "You are related to the famous inventor Mr. Toussaint Kaisin?"

"My father." Joe smiled.

"How wonderful! I hope to meet him someday," she said to him, then turned to Adelina.

Her eyes grew round as they fell to the distended belly and delivered a shocked response to her brother that Joe could only guess at.

To Adelina she said, "My brother said nothing of this news in his letters home." She shot an accusatory glare in Andrew's direction. "Our mother will be very excited to finally meet you."

Adelina reached for Lin Mei's hands. "I'm happy to meet all of you. Don't be upset with Andrew. We wanted it to be a surprise."

"We should get you up to the village before the day grows too hot. It's a long walk, much of it uphill." Ms. Lau again admonished her brother. "We should hire a rickshaw."

"No, please, I'm eager to stretch my legs after so long on board the airship."

"Are you sure?" Andrew turned to her. At her nod, he turned back to Joseph. "You'll join us, won't you? There is always a celebration when I return, but everyone will be involved since Lina is coming to meet my family for the first time."

"They're getting married soon," Ms. Lau beamed.

"I'm afraid I'd be a fish out of water, Andrew. I don't speak the language or know the customs."

"Then I would be in good company, Joe, since I'm quite lacking as well," Adelina said with a laugh. "I will be relying heavily on Andrew and the patience of the Lau family."

"I will help translate. It will be easy. Don't worry." Ms. Lau insisted, smiling at both. "Please, join us."

Joe studied his friend's face. "How could I pass on the opportunity to meet your family? Especially with such lovely ladies in attendance."

Andrew clapped him on the back good-naturedly and took Adelina's carpetbag, then her hand, leading on at her pace.

Ms. Lau refused Joe's offers to carry her crate, but seemed content to walk alongside him, casting him furtive glances.

CHAPTER TWO

—⊰⊱⊰※⊱⊰⊱—

"He is very handsome, isn't he?" Mama handed bowls of steaming rice to Lin Mei, then scowled. "Too young and strong and handsome to be a professor."

Lin Mei jumped, lost in thought, staring at Professor Kaisin. "Maybe," she shrugged and took the bowls from her mother, face averted so she wouldn't see the sudden flush of color.

"Strong like a farmer," Mama said with a decisive nod. "You should talk with him."

"I have been."

"Translating between him and the villagers isn't the same."

Lin Mei stared at her mother with suspicion. "He's leaving when the Soaring Dragon sails."

Mama leveled her eyes at her daughter. "It's just talking. Have some fun." Her gaze slid toward the open door where Andrew and Adelina were visible. A faraway smile curved her lips. "It's good to see him happy."

Lin Mei grunted. "He's been grumpy for too long. Maybe now that he has a baby coming, he'll stop bossing me around."

Mama snorted. "You're just as bossy. And even more stubborn. Put those on a tray and take some vegetables with you. Talk."

"Who's bossy?" Lin Mei grabbed chopsticks and sped away from her mother's playfully upraised soup spoon.

She placed the tray on a low table at Professor Kaisin's knee, where he sat on a stool under the shade of a banyan tree. Pushing aside the discarded teacup, she handed him a pair of the chopsticks and a bowl, then proceeded to load the vegetables into it, ignoring his look of surprise.

Despite the increasing heat, he hadn't removed his jacket or his gloves.

"Thank you, Ms. Lau." He held the chopsticks with a deft hand, waited for her to get her own food, then tucked in.

She smiled.

Most of the westerners she'd met refused to even try the utensils and would demand a fork or a spoon.

She bit into a spinach stalk, trying to think of something to ask him. Since arriving that morning, the villagers had descended on the small group, asking everything under the sun of him and Adelina.

She'd learned a lot.

An unmarried professor, based in England while working around the world. He was in Hong Kong to move his father's household back to Europe, where he could keep an eye on him.

His sister cared for their father in his absence.

It was unusual for an unmarried young man. Usually, daughters were expected to care for ailing parents exclusively.

She glanced at her mother, seated across the courtyard, talking with Andrew and Adelina. Still healthy and independent, and much more animated since they'd arrived with news of the baby coming. That spark had ignited something within their mother that had nearly gone out when their father died.

"Tell me of your father, Mr. Kaisin, I've always wanted to meet him and see some of his inventions," Lin Mei said to the professor. Her gaze swept his handsome features, wishing she could remove his spectacles to better see his blue eyes.

He glanced up at her from the half-empty bowl and smiled. "Call me Joe. Mr. Kaisin is my father. All his inventions are being shipped back to London, along with the partially finished projects from his workshop. You are interested in mechanical inventions, Ms. Lau?"

The dimples that appeared when he smiled momentarily distracted her.

"Oh, yes!" She sat up straighter as the topic flooded her with excitement. "Last year, I went to an exposition on the island, and it was wonderful. Such creativity! And if I call you Joe, you must call me Lin Mei." Color flooded her cheeks as she smiled at him. "I should like to go to London one day. I've read in the newspapers there are expositions for new patents often."

"There are."

"The news of your father's adventures aboard the Soaring Dragon was also all over the newspapers." She glanced at her brother with a frown. "Andrew refused to tell me much about what happened. I had to read about it."

Professor Kaisin laughed. "I'm sure it was a fanciful account. That particular adventure and his declining health is the reason I persuaded him to remain in London with me. His eccentricities get him into far too much trouble. But I am thankful Andrew and Adelina kept him and his patents safe and unharmed from would-be thieves."

"Adelina helped? I didn't realize you were acquainted with her as well. From your early days with Andrew, I suppose?"

He nodded, returning his attention to his bowl, clearing his throat.

"Would you like more tea, Professor?"

He glanced at the sun, then pulled a watch from his pocket. "Thank you, no. I need to return before it gets too late in the day. I'm glad I had the opportunity to finally meet Andrew's family and see his village. He talked about all of you back in our school days. I'd had no idea his sister was so lovely." He stood, taking Lin Mei's hand, and bent over it.

At his touch, Lin Mei's heart raced and skipped, causing her cheeks to flush even more. The scent of his soap and aftershave tickled her nose. When he glanced up into her face, his blue eyes held hers.

Mama is right. Professor Kaisin—Joe—is very handsome.
Her stomach tightened.

And I'll probably never see him again.

She was sorry when his gloved hand finally released hers, but the look in his eyes made her breath hitch. He blinked and it was gone, leaving her to wonder if she'd imagined it.

"YOU'RE NOT LEAVING ALREADY, are you, Professor?" Mrs. Lau approached, carrying a tray with a fresh pot of tea. "Lin Mei hasn't performed for us yet."

"Mother, please," Lin Mei groaned.

"She's pretty good. You might as well stay just a little longer since you'll miss the wedding celebrations." Andrew said, slipping an arm around his sister with a proud smile.

The top of her head barely reached Andrew's shoulder.

Her cheeks flushed and her delicate brows shot up as she looked at her brother.

Curiosity won out. "If Andrew says you're good, then how can I refuse?" Curiosity, and the desire to spend a little more time with her.

His gaze returned to Lin Mei's face, like he couldn't quite get enough of her.

Careful, Joe. She's Andrew's sister.

It couldn't hurt to indulge a little, after all, he was leaving the hemisphere soon.

Andrew shouted across the communal space, wherein an older man jumped to his feet, nodded, and darted into one of the nearby houses.

"Andrew, the new costume I'm making isn't finished," Ms. Lau said, the color in her cheeks deepening over the fuss.

The man returned from his house with a stringed instrument.

"All you need is the music, Lin Mei." Andrew winked at his sister who sighed in defeat and cast a baleful glance at their mother.

Joe couldn't suppress his smile as he reclaimed his seat under the tree to watch Ms. Lau's dance.

She took her position in the center of the open community space, while all the villagers spread out around her, settling in to watch.

Lin Mei looked smaller as she stood alone.

And so still, that a large black-winged butterfly chose her shoulder to rest on, before continuing on its way.

She didn't move a muscle until the first notes of the stringed instrument signaled her start.

Slow, controlled movements, graceful arcs, and light sweeps of her toes chased her shadow over the flagstones.

The butterfly continued on, as did she, eyes closed in absolute focus.

Joe's first impression of Ms. Lau returned as he watched her; she was...*Breathtaking*.

Her hands fluttered, and her body arched before spinning into a leap that reminded him of the passing butterfly.

Joe absorbed every movement, every expression.

Ms. Lau continued to move in perfect flow, short subtle gestures followed by long graceful sweeps.

She returned to her original pose as the music slowed to a final lingering note.

Lifting her head, she opened her shining eyes and smiled. At *him*.

Joe's heart tripped, causing him to suck in a breath he hadn't realized he'd been holding.

He returned her smile and clapped his appreciation.

She dipped her head and turned to bow to the accompanying musician, then her community.

The sun was barely above the western mountain ridge now and the air had cooled significantly.

Joseph said his goodbyes to Mrs. Lau and the villagers, then to Andrew and Adelina.

Andrew shook his hand. "I'll call on you when I return to Hong Kong to wrap things up on the ship." He hesitated. "Are you sure you don't want me to accompany you back to your father's house?"

Joseph shook his head. "No, no, enjoy your family. I'll see you in the next couple of days."

At her mother's behest, Ms. Lau walked him as far as the community hall, directing him to the market where he could find his way back to Hong Kong proper.

"It was good to meet one of Andrew's old friends from school," she said at the junction where they were to part ways.

Joe smiled down at her. "Thank you for that wonderful performance. You dance like..." he searched for the right words. "A butterfly."

Returning his smile, she said, "I hope we meet again someday, Professor. Joe." Before he could say anything else, she turned and hurried back up the path.

He remained fixed until she disappeared around a sharp bend in the road.

The sense of loss prickled over him. Shaking himself, he resumed his journey.

The tug to follow her lingered.

He reflected on his visit to Andrew's ancestral home.

The villagers had been excited about Andrew's arrival and curious about Adelina and himself.

Ms. Lau had patiently translated back and forth, so at ease and lively. Sometimes admonishing, clearly censoring some of their questions.

Joe relished his time with her all day. He'd caught himself searching the villagers' faces for her when she wasn't nearby.

There was still much to be done before the airship set sail. Every time he tried to focus on the incomplete tasks ahead, his thoughts strayed to Ms. Lau.

Lin Mei with her bright eyes, infectious laugh and scent of sweet grass and mountain air.

CHAPTER THREE

"You said yourself that you're staying here, Andrew. Why can't you get me a job on the ship? Just one tour?" Lin Mei's voice rose as she scowled up into her brother's face.

He scowled back. "Mother needs you here. Besides, you can't go off alone."

"I wouldn't be alone, Andrew. I'd be with your co-workers." She grit her teeth, struggling to control her temper.

"That's what I'm afraid of," he muttered. "I wouldn't be there to keep them in line."

"So you'd take me aboard when you go back to work?"

"I didn't say that." A muscle flexed in his jaw.

"I can earn far more working with you on that ship than I could here, no matter how much of Mama's rice wine I sell. You know it."

"Don't you want to settle down on a farm of your own?"

Lin Mei's hands landed on her hips as she stared at her brother, then pointedly slid her gaze to Adelina. "Why don't the two of *you* settle down on a farm while I go off adventuring?"

"I don't go off *adventuring*," he snapped, "It's my job."

Lin Mei lifted her chin. "I want a job, too."

Andrew dropped his voice. "Mother needs you here."

Lin Mei's hands curled into fists at her sides. "No, she doesn't, Andrew. She needs help with income for the little ones. But that doesn't mean she needs *me* here. Besides, even Mama doesn't want to stay in the village for the rest of her life. She wants to open a shop. She needs money for that."

He straightened; his gaze slid toward the house.

Lin Mei glanced back to see Mama and Adelina cleaning and cutting vegetables. Neither of them looked at the arguing siblings. Andrew's eyes were glued to Adelina. He was quiet a long time before he spoke again. "Does Mama know you want to leave?"

"We haven't spoken about it, but she knows. Why do you think she sends me to the harbor?"

Andrew finally turned his full attention back to Lin Mei, suddenly looking sad and tired. "Father spent all his earnings on my education. All that could be spared, and it put him in an early grave. He couldn't set aside money for your dowry to make a comfortable match."

"I don't want a dowry to marry, which is only the best option if I stay here. I want to find a good job to help support our family, too."

"Lin Mei, I have to collect the rest of our belongings from the ship. We'll discuss this later. Maybe we can consider it for when I return to work, and I can keep an eye on you."

Lin Mei sucked in a breath at his dismissal. She doubted a later discussion would be any more progressive. He'd just find another reason to deny her request for help to find work aboard the ship.

Andrew went to speak to Adelina and Mama a moment before he turned toward the road out of the village.

A moment later, Adelina approached, offering Lin Mei a teacup. In her frustration, she was about to decline, then sighed. It wasn't Adelina's fault her brother was so infuriating.

"He's certainly over-protective," Adelina offered.

Lin Mei laughed. "Stubborn."

"You have no idea." Adelina sipped her tea. "You know, most of the crew are good folk. It's usually just the temporary hires that need surveillance. And the passengers."

"You'd think the ship was swarming with lecherous villains, the way he acts."

"Well, he is head of security. It's his job to act that way."

Lin Mei snorted. "There are plenty of such people around here, especially down in the market and the harbor."

"Once you make it on board the ship, you'll fall in love with it." Adelina turned sparkling eyes to Lin Mei. "She has secrets even Andrew hasn't yet discovered."

"Do you think Andrew will allow it?"

Adelina bit her lip. "How much does it mean to you?"

"His approval or the trip?"

"Applies to both."

Lin Mei glanced back toward the house where mother continued to work. Guilt gnawed through her.

"I may not be fluent in Cantonese or Hakka, but I've picked up a few words here and there. And, I have excellent body language skills. I can see how much she loves you. And I can see the regret when she's presented with your obvious longing to leave home."

"She didn't have the chance to choose."

"Maybe. Or maybe she *did* choose. And maybe she's working toward being able to make the choice again."

Lin Mei's gaze found her younger siblings. It would be a long while before the burden of caring for her family would ease. But they were approaching an age they were helping more and more.

"Perhaps." Lin Mei said. "I hope so."

Adelina took Lin Mei's empty cup. "The staff will be occupied with restocking the ship. This is a good time to get a private tour of the ship while it's quiet."

Lin Mei's heart skipped as her gaze sought the road out of the village. Andrew was already out of sight, but it wouldn't take her long to catch up to him.

She grinned at Adelina, gave her hand a light squeeze, and broke into a run.

"I'm going to town with Andrew," she shouted as she passed her mother, not giving her time to object.

LIN MEI STRODE NEXT to Andrew, head high, excitement rippling through her.

He'd stopped arguing with her by the time they'd passed through the market and reached the wharf and ferry depot.

She could barely contain her excitement as they boarded the bustling ferry to cross the harbor.

Andrew cast her a pained glance and sighed.

She grinned at him.

"Stay out of trouble," he said. Again.

"I never get into trouble, Andrew," she countered.

He snorted. "I don't want to see the angry end of Mother's soup spoon if something happens to you."

It was Lin Mei's turn to snort. "Which hasn't happened since the time she caught you smoking behind the temple with the other village boys."

"Just behave," he warned as the ferry's engine slowed.

Disappointed the ride was nearly over, she contented herself, knowing they'd have to ride it again to return home.

Instead, she focused on the impending tour she'd bullied her older brother into.

He led her past the disembarking ferry passengers, around the dockworkers and slowed as they reached the platform under the airship tethered to its mooring mast.

Her breath caught as she stood beneath it, staring up at the bottom of the gondola. The envelope of the balloon shimmered under the strong sun.

"It's even more beautiful up close," she said after she finally drew another breath.

Distracted by her words, he glanced at her, then up at the airship. He smiled. "It is. Wait till you see inside." He winked at her.

Her smile widened.

They moved past tarp-covered cargo toward the mooring mast.

The sound of a growl caught her attention. She turned, listening, moving slowly back along the cargo.

The growl sounded again as she stopped and lifted the edge of a small tarp covering an iron cage. She gasped as a white tiger cub backed into the corner of the cage bars, hissing at her.

"Lin Mei!"

She dropped the tarp at the sound of Andrew's voice and rushed toward the steps that wound up the tower toward the ship. "Coming."

CHAPTER FOUR

JOSEPH STRODE TOWARD THE cargo stacked below the airship. He met with the master stevedore and went over the collection of smaller crates.

While the bulk of the household furniture and his father's larger inventions were going by steamship, he'd been careful to remove key patented components from them to be stored aboard the Soaring Dragon.

Several break-ins had occurred at his father's Hong Kong home after the airship incident. The constabulary had posted officers and guards around the family property until Joe's arrival to clear it out and close it up.

He mounted the mooring mast without looking down or stopping to admire the landscape. He wondered if Andrew and Lin Mei's village was visible from the ship.

From the top of the mast, he crossed the gangplank and breathed a sigh of relief once his feet were firmly inside the gondola of the airship.

It's going to be a long journey, but at least it will be a comfortable one.

He smiled at the visage of the ship's pilot, waiting nearby to greet him.

"Welcome aboard, Professor Kaisin."

"Thank you, Captain Long. I appreciate you taking the time to meet with me. I know you have much to do." He shook the captain's proffered hand.

"It's my pleasure. I have tea prepared in my private quarters." He led Joe away from the ornate entry and along several wood paneled corridors until they reached their destination.

Captain Long indicated two chairs set next to a small table with a tea tray. He poured the steaming brew for both of them, offering one to Joe as he sat.

The personal quarters of the ship's pilot were far more simplistic than Joseph expected them to be. The only ornamentation was in the few antique objects displayed on a small cherry wood shelf next to a simple desk.

Joseph was familiar with the style and age of the objects, as he'd spent the last years traveling around the world cataloging such items for the Crown. His father may have been born in Belgium, but Joe and Clara were British nationals, like their late mother. He bent to inspect a pair of winged dragons embellished with curling clouds, carved in jade. "Exquisite. Warring States period?"

"Yes, indeed," Long said with a nod. "Gifted from my brother. He's interested in antiquities, much like yourself."

"I should like to have a conversation with him some day. That is a wonderful collection you have there." Joe sipped the hot tea. "Have you spoken to my brother-in-law about the investigation into the incident involving my father?"

"Yes, I met with Chief Clayton. I was sorry to hear of your father's ill health. Please extend my good wishes." Captain Long said. "His officers at the Hong Kong police station have been working diligently to determine who was involved with the attempted theft of your father's patents."

Joe nodded. "Thanks to Andrew Lau and Adelina Curren's efforts, both the patents and my father are safe under Crown guardianship."

"In Andrew's absence during this voyage, Daniel Jones will step up for him, at his recommendation." The captain cleared his throat and sipped his tea.

"You don't trust the replacement?"

Captain Long smiled. "Your father and Chief Clayton had been assured of Stevens' reliability before the voyage, and that hadn't turned out so well. I've come to rely on Lau's integrity and ability as my head of security. Do you trust his choice?"

Joe considered before answering. It wasn't his choice to make, but everyone involved understood how valuable his father's work was. "As much as I wish Andrew would be on duty, I am pleased for him and for Adelina that they will be with family to welcome their first child. I must trust his choice." Joe set his half-empty teacup and saucer on the small table next to him. "Michael—Chief Clayton—mentioned he gave you a copy of his report."

Captain Long nodded. "He did. I'm not surprised the Hong Kong gangs were involved in convincing Mr. Stevens to betray his post and try to steal your father's patents. They specialize in intimidation, coercion, burglary, robbery, and often murder. My men have noted their presence and harassment of the dock stevedores. They're becoming bolder."

"Michael posted guards at my father's Hong Kong house after it was burgled several times. Would-be thieves damaged the steel door to his workshop but failed to get beyond it."

"That is good news."

"Witnesses identified several members of a gang known to work for various European nationals. While he's in Hong Kong,

Andrew will continue to work with Michael to deepen their investigation." Joe stood. Extracting a thin wooden box from within his vest, he held it out for Captain Long. "Thank you for taking time out of your schedule. I still have a few things to finalize before we depart."

Captain Long also stood and took the box from Joe with a slight nod and tucked it into his own jacket pocket. "My pleasure. Perhaps we will continue our discussions in the coming weeks."

"I look forward to it. I will see myself out."

"Check in with Jones before you leave the ship."

LIN MEI MARVELED AT the luxury as she followed her brother through the airship. The carved bamboo wood paneled corridors, the massive ornate gilt mirror of the dining hall, the delicate hand-crafted pieces in the rooms. Elegant decor carefully chosen for its lightweight and superior craftsmanship surrounded her.

"I must speak with my colleagues. There's nothing to see along the crew areas of the ship, so you may as well wait here." Andrew left her alone in the empty guest lounge.

She lingered by the expansive windows, absorbing the view of the harbor and the surrounding landscape. A different perspective from the mountaintop view above her village. How beautiful it all was from so high above, looking down on the bustle of the docks and streets leading away from the pier, and the other airships moored nearby.

Would London look just so? The other cities and ports along Soaring Dragon's route?

She loved her home, but longed to soar and see the world for herself, not just relive it through the tales of others.

In the distance, ocean-going vessels floated on the horizon as they came and went from the busy harbor. Fixated on the view, she recalled snatches of conversation she'd overheard from Andrew and Adelina as they whispered about their work. Some of those exchanges had been curious—cryptic.

What had happened during their travels that they held back from her and their mother? Andrew rarely spoke of his work. Not when he was a constable with the local police force, nor now, as the ship's chief of security. Not the important aspects, anyway.

Her gaze fixed on the loading crew moving crates into place below the ship. Craning, she sought the bulk of the covered cage, unable to spot it as the ship bobbed and swayed at its mooring.

Andrew reappeared next to her. "Incredible view, isn't it?"

She started, pressing a hand to her chest. "Does the Soaring Dragon transport animals?"

"Rarely, but yes, under special circumstances. Most large cargo and animals would go by sea.

"Exotic animals too?" She thought of the cage on the dock.

He pulled his watch from his pocket. "As I said, under special circumstances there could be animals so long as they're not large."

"I—."

"Lin Mei, I have one last meeting with the ship's captain before we can go home." Andrew cut her off, focused on a notebook he pulled from his pocket.

Perhaps she could sneak another peek at the cage's occupant before they went home. For now, she contented herself with the brief experience of just being there. Who knew if she'd ever have another chance to be aboard this ship, let alone any other ship ever again.

If my mother has her way, the only vessel I'll ever sail on would be a fishing boat that belonged to my future husband.

She shuddered, drawing a deep breath to dispel the sense of suffocation that gripped her every time she thought about it.

Her eyes prickled and her heart twisted as she stared out of the windows, squinting against the lowering sun.

Now isn't the time for self-pity. Enjoy this while you can, Lin Mei.

"Are you alright?" Andrew's soft voice drew her attention to his concerned face.

"Yes, of course."

"We'll talk later?"

She offered him a smile. "Always." Then she grinned. "Over the best *siu mai* in town."

He mirrored her grin. "Deal. I'm almost finished here." He gave her shoulder a gentle squeeze.

"Take all the time you need. I'm enjoying this." She searched his face. "Thank you for bringing me aboard Soaring Dragon, Andrew."

"I know how much you've wanted to see her."

Maybe someday, if my fisherman husband and I work hard enough, we can go on a voyage too.

He left her to her thoughts by the windows overlooking Hong Kong, lost in the activity. Eventually, she dropped her gaze to the dock below the swaying ship, now cast in lengthening shadows, where the rest of the cargo waited to be loaded. The edge of the covered cage was now visible.

A woman in a dark dress, with a hat perched atop her blond hair, stepped into view, pointing at the cage with a walking stick. A worker lifted the tarp, folding it back over the top. She bent her face close to the bars. A white paw swiped out at her. She jerked back, fingers pressed to her face. She slammed the handle of her walking stick on the top of the cage and gestured toward the worker, who leaped forward to pull the tarp down. The woman stalked away, followed by a plainly dressed woman.

"Hungry?"

"Huh? Oh yes. Starved." Reluctantly, Lin Mei turned away from the windows at the sound of her brother's voice and followed him out into the corridor that led to the gangway.

"Andrew, Ms. Lau, good afternoon."

She turned to see Professor Kaisin approaching from an office. Her heart pattered a little faster at the sight of his handsome face.

"Joe," Andrew said, grinning at his friend. "Lin Mei and I are going to eat. You'll join us?"

Lin Mei watched Professor Kaisin's face, hopeful.

Professor Kaisin's gaze lingered on her before he pulled his watch from his pocket. "I have time before my last meeting."

His blue eyes caught hers again as he leaned, just a little, toward her.

Warmth rippled through her when his dimples reappeared with his smile.

"Good," Andrew said and led the way back down the narrow steps to the dock, putting Lin Mei between the two of them.

CHAPTER FIVE

As the little group reached the bottom of the mast tower, Lin Mei hung back and maneuvered herself so that she walked behind Professor Kaisin and Andrew. Moving alongside the cargo, she paused with a furtive glance and peaked under the cage's tarp again.

The white tiger cub, curled up in the far corner, stared back at her.

"Hello little one. Aren't you beautiful," Lin Mei breathed in Cantonese.

The cub's ears twitched, but it didn't move.

Aside from the cub, the cage was empty. No food. No Water.

"You must be hungry," she murmured.

The cub lifted its head.

Lin Mei cast a glance over her shoulder. Andrew would notice her absence.

"I don't have food now, but I'll come back later," she whispered and dropped the tarp, hoping the cage wouldn't be loaded into the airship before she could return.

She hurried to catch up, heart pounding, skin flushed.

"Are you well, Ms. Lau?" Professor Kaisin asked, concern clear in his eyes.

"Oh yes, just the excitement of finally being aboard the ship."

"That ship is my sister's obsession. She's been after me for months to sneak her aboard. I wouldn't be surprised if she stowed away one day," Andrew said.

"Why should *you* have all the adventures?" Lin Mei straightened her spine.

"I'm not adventuring, Lin Mei. I'm working." Andrew scowled at her.

"Working? Flying all around the world." She rolled her eyes and changed the subject to avoid another *debate* with her brother. How did Adelina put up with him? "Which tea house are we going to? I'm starving."

Andrew grunted and waved an arm up the street. "It isn't far."

JOE'S GAZE FOUND MS. Lau over and over again.

He enjoyed the banter between the two siblings; something that was non-existent between himself and his sister Clara.

"What's so funny, Joe?" Andrew demanded as they settled down at their cramped little table.

A teapot slammed onto the surface, followed by the sharp rattle of thick porcelain dishes and wooden chopsticks.

The table was so small, it was a challenge to find a comfortable position where their knees weren't pressed together as they perched on the low stools.

Joe chuckled. "Nothing... it's just that in all the years I've known you since our school days back in England, I've never seen this side of you."

"What side?"

Lin Mei's knee bumped Joe's under the table.

"You mean the obstinate, bullheaded, argumentative side?" Lin Mei offered as she snatched Joe's dishes and chopsticks to wash them in her bowlful of tea before handing them back to him, sanitized and dripping.

Andrew grunted in response.

Lin Mei grabbed Andrew's dishes and repeated the cleansing process. As soon as she'd finished cleaning her own, she poured the washing tea into a spare bowl on the table.

Andrew picked up the teapot, filling first Joe's cup, then Lin Mei's before his own. He set the pot down, spout facing away from all of them.

Joe tapped the table in thanks, as was the local custom, then sipped the hot Oolong.

"I'm not bullheaded."

Lin Mei snorted.

"I'm inclined to agree with your sister, Andrew. But that's not necessarily a bad thing. With the challenges we faced in school—especially you?" Joe turned to Lin Mei. "Your brother's exemplary stubbornness got him through the hells of aristocratic school life, despite being neither an aristocrat, nor of money—old or new. And most certainly not blending in with everyone else."

"It wasn't easy for you either."

Lin Mei's gaze darted to Andrew's face, studying him.

"What do you want to order?" Andrew craned his neck, looking around the tea house's large room for any available staff members.

"You never let on it was difficult," she said softly, hand touching Andrew's sleeve.

"Why should I? It was an honor to go. I know how hard everyone worked—especially father—for me to have that education."

Lin Mei's throat worked as she held his gaze a moment longer. She squeezed his arm. "I'll have the *siu mai*. Thank you."

He nodded and lifted a hand to signal the server. "Joe?"

Joe named a couple of dishes, then whispered to Lin Mei conspiratorially, "Someday I will regale you with your brother's exploits."

"Then I will have free rein with yours," Andrew said, brow raised.

Joe chuckled again, knowing full well Andrew would never actually tell his little sister about the mischief Joe was involved in. "You'll have to join me for a few drinks when you're in London."

Andrew nodded. "Of course."

Aside from the reminiscing, Joe mused that it would also be a good time to exchange vital information about his father's case and the Crown's expectations.

"Tell me about some of your adventures chasing antiquities," Lin Mei prompted Joe once the food arrived, and she began sharing it out with the communal chopsticks.

Her knee pressed against his again. He didn't move away this time, allowing himself to enjoy the contact, even if for just a little while.

When she finished and glanced up at him with those large luminous eyes of hers, he couldn't suppress a smile.

Smile?

A notion that had become foreign to him in the last few years.

His unexpected reunion with his old friend and introduction to his charming, lively younger sister had him feeling lighter than he had in a very long time. He glanced down at his gloved hands, resisting the urge to squeeze his left hand into a fist, as had become his habit.

Lin Mei didn't carry the gravity that Andrew did.

Where Andrew was serious and brooding, more like himself, Lin Mei was laughter and light and teasing and mischief despite the hardship of growing up in a small village, working all hours to keep themselves fed.

A lifestyle Joe knew nothing about.

He suddenly wished he could spend more time talking to her, despite his own circumstances. His duties to his father and to his work.

"You'd be bored to tears. It's all long hours traveling just to inspect a dusty old artifact, then write reports and contracts and see to the thing's safety as it's shipped back to London."

Relatively speaking—as an antiquities inspector, which he had taken on more of since his sabbatical from the agency.

The fingers of his left hand twitched again.

His work for the Crown was a different matter.

He left out the espionage, the danger to his person and colleagues, and the prisoner transportation and arrest reports.

Andrew was very familiar with those aspects of his work, but Joe suspected he had never told his sister about the agency work he and Adelina did.

No, he'd have to be selective about any stories he told this beautiful young lady during their meal.

Their last meal together.

Joe swallowed down the sudden rise of regret.

He studied her in glimpses. The delicate, quick movements of her hands as she delegated food with the chopsticks. Setting them aside and retrieving her own, she raised a piece of prawn to her plump lips.

His gaze hung on those lips, pink and lush and so quick to smile.

The sense of regret grew heavier as it slid down into his gut.

Stay.

Talk.

Kiss.

Joe turned his attention back to his bowl and the food she'd selected and placed there for him.

What would *she* taste like, where he to kiss her?

Sunshine and light and mountain air.

Visions of kisses and laughter and love making entered his imagination in a way that they hadn't in years.

Not since ... Eleanora.

A chill splashed over Joe, washing away the growing desire.

Ms. Lau was his oldest friend's sister.

He quickly shut away the whimsical thoughts and slammed the door on the lustful ones.

That, would not do.

He moved his knee, breaking the contact.

"I wouldn't," she said.

"Wouldn't what?" he said, realizing he'd lost the thread of conversation.

"Be bored listening to stories of your travels. I'll probably never get to travel and have stories of my own, so I enjoy listening to other people's experiences."

Her tone was light, but Joe didn't miss the hitch in her voice as she said the words.

"I'm sure someday you will."

"No." She sipped her tea. "I'll be too busy raising the children I bear the fisherman-husband mother has lined up for me."

The regret piled like boulders in his gut. He glanced up at Andrew.

Andrew shrugged. "He's a good match. Works hard, is dutiful to his family, and is kind. As are the others that Mother has in mind for Lin Mei."

Jealousy reared in Joe's chest.

I'm dutiful and hardworking.

Joe wouldn't say he was kind, but he did have a soft spot for children and animals.

Then he shoved all of those thoughts aside too.

Don't be ridiculous, Joseph.

But he couldn't help himself as he watched Lin Mei.

Ms. Lau, he reminded himself.

He pulled the watch his father had made for him from his pocket. "I should be going. Thank you for the meal." He rose from his stool, then gave Ms. Lau a slight bow. "A pleasure to speak with you again."

To Andrew he added, "Send me a note next time you're in London and we'll have those drinks."

"I will." Andrew stood, shaking Joe's hand. "Take care of yourself."

"Same to you. Both of you. Ms. Lau." Joe bowed his head and left, ignoring Lin Mei's surprised expression.

"That was abrupt. Did I say something wrong?" He heard Ms. Lau ask Andrew as Joe left the small tea house.

"No. He just has a lot on his mind."

Joe kept going as though he hadn't heard the exchange.

The regret in his gut inched a little bigger.

The urge to return to the table, even for just five more minutes with his friend and with Lin Mei, dragged at him.

He ignored it as he strode through the darkened streets toward his last meeting before he left Hong Kong.

CHAPTER SIX

WHILE ANDREW WAS DISTRACTED arguing with the server over the bill, Lin Mei shuffled extra food into a linen square she kept in the bag she always carried. She tucked the bundle away, hoping he wouldn't notice.

She'd promised a certain tiger cub she'd return.

When Andrew turned his attention back to the table, he glanced at her with suspicion.

"I might get hungry later," she said with a shrug.

"I'm sure you will. Why do you look as though I caught you planning to do something you oughtn't?"

She rose from her seat and shrugged. "How should I know why you're so suspicious of everyone?"

His eyes narrowed on her.

"Shall we go? I think mother said she needed another jug of cooking oil."

"Cooking oil? That shop is some distance from here." He glanced at the setting sun, then his pocket watch. The sun rested on the nearby rooftops before its final descent. "I will go. You go home before it gets too dark. I'm going to visit with Chief Clayton while I'm here."

She immediately bristled at the dismissal, then relaxed. This would make it easier for her to see the cub again without his interference.

"See you at home." She started off for the dock.

"Don't linger, Lin Mei. Go straight to the ferry. The docks are no place for you after dark."

She turned back toward her brother. "You're home just a few days and already you're back to bossing me around like when we were children. I'm an adult now and can take care of myself."

He scowled and shook a finger at her. "Straight home."

She rolled her eyes and resumed her path. "Yes, elder brother."

She rounded a corner and ducked alongside the wall, pressing herself close to peer around it back the way she'd walked, and breathed a sigh of relief.

In the distance, Andrew strode up the hill in the direction of the police station.

Heart pounding in her chest, she spun and ran toward the loading dock below the moored Soaring Dragon.

Please, let it still be there!

She made her way around the airship's cargo. Most had been loaded, still more awaited—including the cage.

She drew a deep breath and smiled.

Good.

A man dressed in uniform strode past the cage.

She ducked back into the shadows, suppressing a groan.

Of course there is security, Lin Mei.

That was her brother's role aboard the ship. She'd been too excited at the promise of touring the ship to notice the security detail before.

While she wasn't there to steal anything, she also didn't want to be seen in case they told Andrew.

She loved her brother, but sometimes his fierce protectiveness of their family was overwhelming. When their father died, the role fell heavily on Andrew's shoulders.

While he was gone, she'd taken over some of his duties helping their mother with the sale of their produce.

Lin Mei loved this, being in the city.

The freedom.

She'd long been jealous of her older brother's freedom to come and go as he pleased. To go off and study in Europe, to work aboard a fancy airship.

Why shouldn't I be able to do those things too?

Because society deemed she mustn't.

She snorted and straightened her shoulders.

What society didn't know... society didn't know—and needn't know.

Glancing around for more lookouts, she crept alongside the stacked crates.

She froze when a booming voice called out, then relaxed, realizing it wasn't directed at her, but at someone high above.

Her stomach sank. Anyone up there would see her creeping around like a thief—if they weren't too focused on their work.

Monitoring the dock workers overhead, as well as on ground level, she made her way to the cub's cage set atop a larger crate. She lifted the corner of the canvas covering, then scooted close enough to extend the canvas over herself.

Lin Mei's heart melted. She swallowed down any instinctive noises rising in her throat to coo at the baby before her.

Rounded, fuzzy ears perked forward, and huge unblinking blue eyes stared back at her. Nose and whiskers twitched as the cub scented her.

Her fingers desperately itched to stroke the white and black fur.

Would it bite her?

With difficulty she dismissed the desire to cuddle the fuzzy little feline, lest it maul her face.

But it would be worth it.

"I brought you food," she whispered, noting the cage remained empty around the cub. "Are you hungry?"

The cub didn't move.

Lin Mei reached into her bag, extracted the food she'd hidden away and unwrapped it. "I'm Lin Mei. I wonder what they call you?" she murmured.

The cub's nostrils opened and closed in such a way that Lin Mei knew it was scenting the food.

Withdrawing the shrimp dumplings and roast pork chunks from the napkin, she extended her hand through the bars of the cage. She dropped the food, then pulled her hand away.

The cub lunged forward with a growl, slapping the bars of the cage in front of Lin Mei's face with fuzzy baby paws, forcing her to jerk backward.

The cub hissed its displeasure at her invasion of its limited space, then backed away, casting glances at the food.

Heart racing, Lin Mei couldn't help the smile that teased her lips. The cub as it sniffed, then ate the food, still growling, its vivid blue eyes leveled on her.

Adoration bubbled up through Lin Mei.

She'd never seen anything so wild, beautiful, and wonderful. Magical.

Were it a full-grown tiger, she doubted she would have ever dared what she did now.

Of course I would. I'd just keep a little more distance.

Food devoured; the cub sniffed the floor, seeking more.

"Poor little thing. Haven't they fed you?" she whispered.

The cub's ears twitched, while its head tilted as though trying to comprehend Lin Mei's words.

Lin Mei extracted another bit of food from the napkin and carefully placed it inside the cage, a little closer to the bars.

Slowly this time, the cub approached, eyes flicking warily between Lin Mei and the food placed between them.

A loud crash followed by shouts sent Lin Mei wheeling backward, tripping over abandoned tools. She slammed back against a stack of crates, eyes scanning her surroundings. Whatever had happened was over by the next dock. Drawing a breath to steady her nerves after the fright, she lifted the canvas cover which had dropped. The cub was back in its corner, eyes wide, growling, food abandoned.

"It's alright, little one, you're safe. Come and finish your food," she cooed, heart still pounding. After what seemed like an age, the cub approached the scattered dumplings. Lin Mei's heart twisted as she watched the baby tiger. "Where is your family? You must be so afraid, being all alone here."

She sighed, watching as it licked its lips, sniffing around. Eventually, the cub set about cleaning its face with a fuzzy paw and a stuttered purr.

Lin Mei's smile stretched wide as her heart lifted.

The cub approached, twisted and rubbed its head along the bars in front of Lin Mei. Her hand darted out, gently stroking the soft fur exposed between the bars. "You shouldn't be in here."

The urge to set the cub free overwhelmed Lin Mei, so that her chest felt as though it would burst. The cub allowed the contact, pressing into her hand, reveling in the feel of her fingers rubbing behind its ears.

Tears sprang to Lin Mei's eyes as reality extinguished the building fantasy. "But there's nothing I can do for you, little one."

They would load the cage on the airship soon, since it was scheduled to set sail later that night.

A chill rippled through her. She glanced up, noticing the surrounding space was much darker now. Slowly, she withdrew her hand, relinquishing her connection to this little animal. "I'm sure you'll be fine. Treasured. Spoiled till you're too fat to move."

She gave the cub a last pat and a wide smile. "It was a pleasure to meet you. Safe journey." She backed away from the cage, allowing the canvas cover to fall back into place.

"*Shi shi*."

Lin Mei blinked. That sounded like a child. That also sounded like it came from the cage.

But that couldn't be.

She glanced around the darkness. This wasn't a place for children. From her position in the shadows, she couldn't see anyone other than the stevedores at their work and the patrolmen still in the distance.

Lin Mei couldn't explain why she lifted the canvas again. Maybe it was just for one last glimpse of the adorable little cub.

It wasn't a cub that stared back at her in the darkness.

A small naked girl, sitting on her knees, stared back. "*Shi shi*."

The cub was gone.

Lin Mei blinked, lungs frozen.

The canvas dropped with a *whoosh* as Lin Mei fell back into the crates behind her, much harder this time.

"*Diel!*" she swore.

She gasped, rubbing her eyes.

It's late. It's dark. I'm tired.

Her fingers stretched toward the canvas. Another breath. Then another. She jerked the cover upward.

"*Shi shi,* Lin Mei." The little girl with striking blue eyes giggled with her tiny hands over her mouth.

Lin Mei's knees buckled. Her throat closed, blocking air to her lungs for a building scream as the air around the girl wavered and blurred her form in the darkness. Seconds later, the air, or Lin Mei's vision—she couldn't be sure which it was, as she couldn't be sure of anything in that moment—cleared.

The cub returned, staring back with perked ears and laughter in her blue eyes.

BARONESS VON SCHLIEFFEN SIPPED her champagne as she looked out of her second-floor window.

Bored.

"Read it to me again, Hermina." She scowled at the rickshaw rattling along the street below. "And speak up this time. The noise outside is insufferable."

"My Lisabeta, I miss your generous, milky white—," her companion began with a high, clear voice.

"Skip that part," the baroness snapped. "Get to the lines about the business. The progress report."

Hermina Engle's lips moved as she skimmed through the letter to the correct passages. "The menagerie is progressing and the holding cell for your newest gift is ready. Work continues for our next acquisitions. We eagerly await your arrival to move onto the next stages of our experiments. Success is near, my love."

"Good. That is good." The baroness nodded. "Dismissed."

Hermina placed the letter next to the baroness' champagne bottle, bobbed and backed to the door before exiting without a sound.

The baroness's attention was elsewhere. With her lover.

"Abelard," she breathed.

Another sip from her champagne flute.

She sauntered her way around the room to retrieve her letter.

Just a matter of weeks now. Weeks before she was back in his arms. Weeks before they could resume their work.

And her prized new pet was the key to its completion.

Weeks. *Just* weeks.

Returning to the window, her gaze found the airship swaying at its mooring. She detested traveling. It gave her indigestion and made her irate. It was unseemly but necessary.

The summit had gone well.

Turning back to the mantle, the clock ticked. Mere hours before she needed to board the floating contraption.

Recalling that she'd dismissed her maid, she reached for the champagne bottle to refill her glass.

It would be worth it.

A frisson swept through her shoulders and down her spine.

They were nearly finished.

CHAPTER SEVEN

LIN MEI'S HEAD SPUN as she stared into the dark cage.

That didn't happen. It couldn't have.

What do I do? What should I do? What could *I do?*

Her gaze slid to the ornate padlock that secured the cage door.

Lin Mei.

She'd heard her name. She shook her head, drawing several deep breaths.

You're mistaken. It's a tiger cub, not a child. Look. Look at those blue tiger eyes, fuzzy fur and swaying tail.

Calm returned. The tremors in her hands eased.

Maybe the Siu Mai was going off...

"Finish loading these crates. It's almost departure time." A nearby dockworker shouted.

Lin Mei crouched to sneak away.

I'm already going to be in trouble for returning home after dark.

Footsteps approached.

Lin Mei squeezed into a space between stacked crates, peering out at two dockworkers approaching to assess the cargo.

"What are we to do with the cub, boss?"

"Load it in the hold with everything else. Feed and water it just enough every few days to keep it alive. They want it docile," the boss said, flicking the edge of the tarp up to look at the cub.

Shouldn't they keep it healthy for the zoo or menagerie it's going to? The other man leaned toward the cage.

"It's bound for a private residence, some aristocrat. Rumor is that it's going to an experimental laboratory."

"Shame."

"Yes, well, your job is to see that it arrives alive. Stay invisible. You're just a servant to them." The boss dropped the edge of the tarp to secure it.

Lin Mei shifted her posture to see the men better in the dark. Her tunic caught on the edge of an abandoned crowbar set on a low crate. It clattered to the ground before she could catch it.

"What was that?"

"Probably just a rat. Here, hold this rope while I secure the hooks. This cage and those crates are the last of the cargo." The two men worked quickly. As soon as they finished, the boss signaled for the cage to be lifted.

It lifted with a jerk and slowly turned.

The cub growled and cried.

Lin Mei's heart lurched as she swallowed against the rising urge to *do* something.

It's just a tiger cub being shipped to Europe. It'll grow fat in some aristocrat's manor house.

Hadn't the dockworker said it was to be experimented on?

She glanced between the two dark figures, still unable to see their features obscured under hats.

What can I do?

She balled her fists against the compulsion to save the cub.

Andrew would be furious if I interfered with someone's property.

It wouldn't change anything. I'd just be in trouble and the cub would be gone. Besides, what would I do with a tiger cub?

"Lin Mei!"

Lin Mei blinked and looked up. In a small gap in the tarp, two little fists clutching the bars were visible.

"Lin Mei!" a little voice wailed.

She stepped out of her hiding place. "Stop! There's a child in that cage. Stop!" Panicked words spilled out of her mouth before thoughts formed. "By the order of the Hong Kong Police, lower that crate!"

The two figures spun in her direction.

"Who the hell are you?" the boss demanded.

She shoved aside the encroaching images of her brother's angry face. "I'm... Uhm—."

"Boss, she was with that constable and the aristocrat earlier today."

"Lau? Damn. She's a spy."

"I'm not a spy, but there's a child in that cage!" she said frantically, looking from the men to the rising cargo.

"We don't have time for this. Shut her up," the boss said.

Lin Mei gaped, heart pounding.

The other man bore down on her as she drew a breath to scream. His hand clamped over her mouth, his arm went around her shoulders, locking her in place.

Shock froze Lin Mei's limbs.

"We don't have time to get rid of her properly. Load her into a crate and dump her once the airship is far out over the ocean. We can't have anyone causing troubles for our employers. We're paid to be invisible and ensure things run smoothly."

"But she said there's a kid—."

Lin Mei's body lurched into action, struggling against her captor. Unable to scream, she wriggled, trying to drive her elbows into his ribs while alternately stomping his feet and driving her heels into his shins.

The much larger dockworker grunted at her efforts, tightening his grip.

"It's an animal. You saw it for yourself. Do your job." The boss barked at his subordinate. "Don't kill her yet. Find out how much she and the cops know first, before you get rid of her."

The steely arm locked around Lin Mei's throat, restricting her ability to breathe.

She fought harder, but blackness overtook her.

JOSEPH INSPECTED HIS ROOM aboard the Soaring Dragon. These quarters were to be his home for the next two months.

A narrow berth against one wall, a tall bamboo stand supporting a fine porcelain washbasin and pitcher in the corner with a small mirror braced above it. A delicate table and matching chair occupied the last bit of wall space, which was covered in beautifully painted wallpaper.

It wasn't much, but it was all intricately carved and richly upholstered.

Checking his pocket watch, Joseph considered his options for the evening.

Thirty minutes to departure. Best change for dinner.

He wasn't the least bit hungry after his late meal with Andrew and Ms. Lau, but his presence would be expected. It would also provide an opportunity to study his fellow passengers.

His father's previous experiences remained at the forefront of Joe's mind. He had to be ready for *when*, not *if*, someone attempted to access his father's patents and key components.

Joe had to remain vigilant.

It's going to be a long, long voyage.

He sighed as he removed his gloves, dropping them on a nearby chair, then loosened his cravat and shirt buttons. Placing his jacket on the back of the chair, he rolled up his shirt sleeves, preparing to wash his face and neck.

He allowed his thoughts to return to the charming Ms. Lau, reminding him of his old friend during their school days.

Bright eyed, with a mischievous glint for trouble—once he'd got to know him.

Now, they were both much too serious for folly-filled adventures. Not since they'd seen more of the world and its plethora of villains.

Does Ms. Lau know how brave her brother is? Or Ms. Curren?

He suspected not.

Just as he'd never shared his work as a crown agent with his former fiancée, he doubted Andrew would share such stories with his family.

It's good he and Adelina have each other. And bloody lucky for Andrew that he saw sense enough to mend their relationship.

Joseph sighed, retrieving the towel to dry his face.

Not that he knew the specifics of their troubles, but he could guess.

Eleanora's lovely face came to mind. Curly blond hair, pale blue eyes, dainty, fashionable, with perfect manners.

Delicate London flower.

Foolishness.

Andrew and Adelina understood each other—understood the life.

Eleanora never would have understood.

Would Lin Mei?

Joe cleared his throat, dispelling that surprise thought.

You don't even know if you're going back to that life at all, Joe.

He glanced down at the rolled sleeves, exposing his forearms. One, his natural limb, still strong from worked muscle, the skin tanned and covered in hair. The other, stronger still, made of gears and intricately woven strands of tempered metals.

Both arms flexed as he curled his hands into fists. His mechanical workings were as silent as his natural muscle. His father's work truly was world class.

He squeezed his left hand into a fist.

Will I ever be used to it?

Joseph sighed, unrolling and re-buttoning his sleeves and collar before reaching for his jacket.

It was for the best that Eleanora broke off their engagement.

He was glad he'd never told her what his true work was. It wasn't like he could endanger her by having her accompany him when he returned to the agency after the *accident*.

Again, *if* he returned to the agency.

He glanced at the narrow berth and then at his mechanical hand.

Agency work is lonely work. And dangerous. They did warn us.

Retrieving his valise from the floor, he placed it on the bed, removed the personal articles and the false bottom so that he could inspect his equipment.

Listening and recording devices, multi-lens goggles, grappling hooks and lines, spare reinforced vest and boots, weapons, and more.

He checked through each one, despite having serviced each piece as he finished packing that morning.

Below that false bottom was another, hiding some of his father's documents.

Tucking away various pieces of defensive equipment on his person, he adjusted the set of his vest and chain supporting his pocket watch.

With a last glance at the time, he grabbed his hat and set off to explore the ship, check his cargo, and meet his neighbors for the journey.

CHAPTER EIGHT

LIN MEI'S BODY VIBRATED, while her head ached.

An engine? A very large one by the feel.

Cracking her eyes open, there was only more darkness, with thin lines of light seeping through, indicating that she was in a box of some kind. Straw poked through her clothes and made her skin itch.

But that wasn't what had awoken her.

Voices.

The memory of her last conscious moments illustrated the dire situation she was now in, clearing away the disorientation.

Trapped.

On board a vessel? The Soaring Dragon? Or perhaps some other ship?

She couldn't be sure, as she resisted the need to stretch her cramped muscles, in case her captors were nearby.

"Our employers won't be pleased," a muffled female voice said.

"There wasn't time to plan how to dispose of her, before."

Lin Mei recognized one of the men's voices from the dock, though neither voice was clear from inside the crate and over the sounds of the ship's engine.

"So you're going to keep her aboard the ship?"

"Of course not," he snarled. "I'm going to get rid of her over the ocean before we reach Singapore."

Lin Mei's heart stopped as she swallowed a surge of panic.

"She could be a crown agent. There were rumors one was embarking on this ship. Question her first to find out what she knows."

Crown Agent?

Lin Mei held her breath, straining to hear above the engine noise and her pounding heart.

"And the boss thought she could be a spy for the constabulary. Or she's just a dock waif looking for something to steal. It isn't easy getting in and out of here unguarded, ma'am."

"I'm aware. The crew thinks we're having an illicit affair," the woman said, voice pinched. "We'll continue the charade. When I check back in a few days' time, I expect answers for our employers, lest *we* be the ones disposed of over the ocean. And make sure you feed that fleabag. It's on you if it dies. I hate cats."

The man grunted.

"Obtain the information and get rid of her long before we reach Singapore. When you do, you will be given a message to wire at port before you resume your duties."

"Yes, Ma'am."

"Ensure you clean up your mess properly. Otherwise, the displeasure of our employers will affect your boss, who I hear can be quite creative in his ruthlessness."

"Yes, he can."

"Good. You understand. Now if she tries to alert the crew to her presence, kill her immediately. But I imagine if she's a waif, as you say, she wouldn't want to be found and arrested by them either. Singapore prisons are equally ruthless, are they not?"

"They are, Ma'am—someone's coming."

"Come closer."

There were sounds of scuffling and moaning.

"I say! No one is supposed to be in here," a new man said.

"You won't tell anyone, would you sir?" the woman said, breathless. "I couldn't bear the shame of losing my position. I have a family to support."

"Perhaps you should think of that before engaging in such... activities. Leave here before I bring in the ship's head of security to deal with you. If I catch you in here again, you'll spend time in the ship's brig."

Lin Mei thought she heard two sets of footsteps leave the area. The third strolled along, checking crates and muttering to himself about undignified behavior aboard such a dignified ship.

"Ah, there, aren't you an adorable little creature," he cooed.

A snarl and a hiss followed.

Lin Mei's heart leapt.

The cub? Am I on the Soaring Dragon?

"I would be cranky being trapped in such a cage, myself."

Lin Mei remained curled up, frozen in indecision. Should she make a noise to draw his attention? What if that woman was right? If they didn't believe she was abducted, they'd just arrest her and send her to prison. What would happen to the girl-cub? No one would believe she wasn't just a tiger cub.

That would get Lin Mei sent to an asylum.

As she lay in the darkness of her box, considering her options, the newcomer finished his inspection of the place and departed. The thin cracks of light disappeared.

She lifted her head, straining to hear any further noises above the engine and her pulse in the blackness.

Nothing.

She dropped her head back.

Heavens, Lin Mei, what have you gotten yourself into this time?

Serious trouble, that's what.

That first man is going to come back and throw you in the ocean.

She slid her hands around the upper portion of the box, pressing and pushing.

Secured shut.

With any luck, the men would have been in too much of a hurry to do a thorough job, since they hadn't tied her up.

She set about trying to find leverage to push the lid free... to no avail.

Just keep trying.

SEVERAL DAYS INTO THE journey, Joseph stood by the large gilt mirror at the entrance to the dining lounge, surveying the spread of guests before him.

Mainly European aristocrats, peers and dignitaries. Several North American barons and a few Asian diplomats.

Jones, Andrew's replacement, was doing an admirable job maintaining an air of security aboard the ship, though Joe could only guess at how busy he was. Ships, like estates and hotels, were like miniature cities, where all manner of things could and would occur, requiring deft professional hands at a moment's notice.

At the thought of Andrew, Joe's thoughts drifted to Lin Mei, as they had done so often since their brief time together before his departure.

"A table, sir?" The concierge stepped alongside Joseph, gesturing toward an empty table by the bank of windows, displaying a breathtaking vista.

Lin Mei would love that view.

Despite the glorious sunset filling the windows, Joseph nodded toward a table set at the back of the room. "Perhaps that one."

"Of course." The concierge led Joseph to the requested table, seated him, then returned to his post once a servant approached.

"*Bo-lay, m'goy.*"

The dining lounge was so much calmer and more spacious than the tea house where their knees had pressed together around the tiny table.

The servant nodded and returned moments later with the requested beverage. As soon as the servant departed with his order, Joe poured the tea. His gaze swept the room, looking for familiar faces. He considered each, cataloging known to unknown. A fair ratio, thanks to his father's connections, his work at the university and time on assignment for the crown.

At the head of the room, curtains slid aside to reveal a small stage occupied by a cluster of musicians. There was no singer to accompany them in Adelina's absence.

Sipping the hot brew, he studied each table grouping until his attention settled on a tall, expensively dressed woman with a narrow face and dramatically up swept blond hair. Her gaze flicked to him several times before she smiled and nodded her head in acknowledgment.

He tipped his, in kind.

By the time his steaming food arrived, he'd noted that several guests studied him with equal interest.

A dark-haired man, seated alone like himself, scowled in his direction from the opposite corner of the dining room.

Two elderly women with a much younger woman between them smiled openly while the younger averted her gaze completely. The high color in her cheeks gave her away.

He averted his too, before the matchmaking could take hold.

... Lin Mei...

Had she made her choice? A farmer? She'd been averse to the fisherman.

He huffed, dispelling the inevitably re-routed thoughts back to Lin Mei again.

Focus, Joe.

A familiar, pretty face framed by wild chestnut curls stared at him with sparks in her eyes and a wry curve to her mouth. She raised her cup to him before taking a sip.

Damn.

Delilah Winter.

Trouble. His fingers tightened on his cup. He set it down before he could damage it.

What is she *doing here?*

She also set her cup down, rose from her seat, and made her way straight to his table.

Joe sighed.

Bold as always.

Before he could stand, a servant appeared from nowhere to pull out a chair for her as she claimed a seat at his table.

"Joe." She greeted him with a twinkle in her eye.

"Ms. Winter." He inclined his head in greeting to the Canadian ex-pat.

"Fancy meeting you here."

"Indeed. On assignment?" He kept his voice low.

"Was. Closed a case back in Victoria, British Columbia, before I caught a ship to Hong Kong."

His eyes narrowed on the vibrant woman.

"Don't worry, Joe." She tapped his forearm with familiarity. "I am tracking someone, but that someone isn't you. Though God knows I ought to be, for some of those shenanigans you pulled back in New York."

He cleared his throat. "Yes, well—,"

"I know. Conflicting missions...and a lifetime ago. You did what you had to, right?" Though she tried to mask the brittleness in her voice, Joe knew her too well. She glanced toward the windows.

"Right." He swallowed the regret before it could rise up and drag his memories down into a dark place he didn't want to go.

When she turned her gaze back to him, her eyes were clear, and her expression controlled.

I'm sorry.

"No hard feelings." She grinned in a way that made him highly suspicious of the spirited, 'sometimes' agent.

"None?" He arched a brow.

"Not at the moment." She winked and rose from her barely warmed seat. "Not at the moment, but I'll see you around the ship."

He watched her leave with some relief, then noticed that more than half of the other guests that hadn't paid attention to him before were now focused on him.

So much for keeping a low profile for as long as possible.

Ms. Delilah Winter had just drawn the attention of every guest on the ship straight to him.

What the hell is she up to now?

CHAPTER NINE

IT HAD TAKEN LIN Mei some time to wedge the crate open and crawl out, earning herself considerable scrapes and bruises and one very serious gash from the splintered wood.

She'd found several reserve barrels of wine, beer and water stored at the back of the cargo hold. Thankfully, they each had bronze taps attached for easy access, wherein she limited herself to small amounts of water.

In the next few days hiding in the cargo hold, Lin Mei had learned that Ming was the cub's name, and that she preferred her tiger form, though she would change shape on the rare occasion she wished to communicate with Lin Mei, which still could be challenging.

Ming spoke Mandarin while Lin Mei spoke Cantonese. Luckily, she'd been exposed to many languages over the years that she had worked near the harbor, selling her mother's rice wine and other wares.

She and the cub got by.

And through all of that, she'd had ample time to weigh her options.

She continued to do so now, as she stared at little Ming in her cage, her fingers rubbing absently on the mending injury.

She dropped her gaze to the healing wound.

When she'd finally escaped from the crate, Lin Mei had lain on the floor, panting and bleeding, until Ming called her name, arms extended through the cage bars, crying.

The cage was set on top of another large crate, as it had been on the pier.

Rousing herself, Lin Mei crawled over and propped herself against the crate until she could pull herself up to stand.

"Hurt," she had said in Mandarin. Ming sniffled, reaching for Lin Mei's hand, pulling it between the bars toward herself.

The air around Ming shimmered as she changed form, her tiny hands turned to paws, holding Lin Mei's arm down.

To Lin Mei's shock, the tiger cub began to lick at the blood over her wound. "No, don't eat me!"

She struggled to pull her arm free, but in Ming's tiger form, she was stronger than a little girl her size ought to be.

She growled, putting more pressure on Lin Mei's arm as she continued to lick.

As Ming's tongue rasped over the torn flesh, Lin Mei realized with a mix of horror and awe that she was cleaning the seeping blood away.

A moment later, the pain receded.

She could only stare as the wound began to knit itself together under Ming's ministrations.

Dieu! They will definitely send me to an asylum.

Tears sprang to her eyes as she stared at the cub-child.

Now, there was just a pink scar under the torn and stained sleeve.

Lin Mei had scrambled back into her original crate to hide during the one instance that the servant had returned to give Ming food and water under the supervision of a security staff.

She'd watched through the cracked lid as he'd cast surreptitious glances in her direction.

From a silver chain slung around his neck, he unlocked the cage to place small bowls of food and water.

Ming rushed forward, lapping at the insignificant portions.

She hadn't finished when the man barked at her, shoved her back, and scooped up the dishes. He scowled in Lin Mei's direction as he re-locked the cage, then left with the security guard.

Lin Mei listened hard for the sounds of the cargo room door's lock sliding into place before she scrambled back out of the crate.

"He'll be back," she said to Ming. "As long as the guard is watching him, we're safe."

I'll be safe.

They have no intention of hurting Ming. Yet.

Exhausted, hungry and dehydrated, Lin Mei slumped against the cage, one hand nestled under Ming's warm, furry body, the other stroking her fur while she slept.

She passed the hours daydreaming. Often about Joe's lovely blue eyes and attractive dimples. Her mother had said he looked far too strong to be just a professor. Lin Mei agreed as she imagined him without his jacket, in just his shirtsleeves.

What would it be like to kiss him?

She was sure it would be pleasant.

Other times, she worried that he was somehow involved with Ming's abduction and imprisonment.

Most often, she tried to figure out ways to escape with Ming.

Ming craved her nearness and comfort.

What can I do? Who could I trust with such a thing? Who would believe me?

Her abductors' words and those of the woman returned to her mind again and again, cycling through her indecision on what to do.

No one would believe me.

Stay hidden in the cargo hold with Ming, bang on the door and scream for help, or try to plead with whomever came for her and convince them she just wanted to return to her village.

So much for the adventurous spirit she thought she had.

Ming was quite clear that she would not become a human child while strangers were around.

So even if she could find someone sympathetic enough to listen, as soon as she told them the tiger was also a human—that could heal, they wouldn't hesitate to lock her in the brig then send her to an asylum.

And yet, it was only a matter of time before that man returned to dump her overboard.

That man worked for someone. Did that someone know that Ming could change form? Was that why they'd taken her?

Professor Joseph Kaisin's father was an inventor. He would need to experiment for the sake of his inventions.

Does the Professor know everything about his father's work?

"Please don't let the cage belong to Professor Kaisin. I couldn't bear it," she whispered, listening to Ming's gentle purring as she slept.

What would Andrew do? He's a trained police constable. He'd know what to do.

What of Professor Kaisin? He and Andrew were good friends... but that was many years ago.

He could help me, maybe, but what of Ming? Surely Professor Kaisin would contact Andrew and have me sent home.

Ming would be alone and vulnerable to her abductors.

How can I protect the child as an animal? Who would care? Nobody. I can't.

Footsteps beyond the door drew Lin Mei's attention from her spiraling thoughts.

Ming's ears twitched.

The sound of the lock being disturbed sent Lin Mei scrambling back toward her crate, but her weakened state slowed her muscles from reacting.

Heart pounding, she heard the door open, voices, then the door quickly closed again, blocking out the sounds.

A moment later, Lin Mei was yanked backward by brutal hands. Hard fingers clamped over her mouth, stifling her cry of surprised pain.

Ming's growls and hissing earned her a hard thump on the top of her cage.

"Quiet," the man growled back, retracting his fist. Ming had swiped his hand with her tiny claws, drawing blood.

Ming backed into the corner of her cage, ears flat, maintaining a steady growl as her blue eyes followed his movements.

Lin Mei's fear set her heart racing.

This is it. He's going to throw me overboard now.

Her gaze darted to the outer cargo door opposite the one he'd entered through.

Maybe being arrested is better than death, no matter how harsh the prisons—or asylums—are.

The man turned Lin Mei around and shoved her up against the crates. "I will hurt you if you make any noise to alert the crew." He was so close, his hot breath crawled across her face before he shook her. "Do you understand?"

She nodded her head, while trying to control her gasping.

Stay calm, Lin Mei. Think.

There was nowhere else to go. One door led to security, the other to the ocean far below.

"Who are you working for?" he demanded as he dragged her closer to the loading door.

She shook her head. Vocal cords closed up, her gaze rooted to the larger door.

He shoved her hard against the crates, his forearm across her throat and shoulders, as he released her mouth.

"No one. I work for my mother selling wine at the hotel beside the harbor."

"We saw you with Police Constable Lau. You're an informant for him, aren't you?"

She shook her head.

"A crown agent, then. You were spying on us at the dock."

Crown agent?

"No, no, I just went to visit the tiger cub and bring her food. That's all. I just want to go home. Please let me go."

His scarred face creased as he grinned. "Sure."

He won't.

Fear faded. Instinct surged, fueling her limbs.

Unable to loosen his grip on her, she drew a deep breath to scream.

A hard blow deflated the attempt.

Her head rang and swam, and her knees buckled from the impact.

He shoved her back against the crate again, forcing her head up, shaking her.

"What do you know? Who did you tell about our business?" he growled into her face again.

"Nothing," she mewled, unable to focus. Dimly, she heard Ming's yowls as she thumped into the bars of her cage. "It's alright," she breathed through numb lips to the little one, to calm her.

"Nothing?" He hauled her closer to the cargo bay door. With one hand, he removed the bar securing it, then shoved it open.

Humid, salted air rushed into the room.

There was nothing beyond that door but wide open sky and rolling ocean below.

Despite the pounding of Lin Mei's heart, calm descended over her.

He really is going to throw me out.

He doesn't want to be discovered any more than I do.

Prison is better than death.

Her knee jerked upward, slamming into his groin. Just as her mother had told her to do if she ever found herself unable to dissuade a persistent suitor.

He wheezed, struggling to control her movements as she gave into her instincts to fight him.

She filled her lungs and screamed.

He hit her again, but it was too late.

CHAPTER TEN

JOE CLOSED THE DOOR to his room, intent on one of his daily strolls about the ship.

He began the regimen for exercise and to keep watch over the ship. He trusted security, but as a crown agent, monitoring events and people around him was too deeply ingrained to ignore.

Moving along the narrow corridor, he heard the distinct laughter of the Baroness Von Schlieffen, whom he'd met on an earlier tour. Opting to avoid the woman, he turned down one of the dimly lit halls used by the servants.

A rough-looking man crossed Joe's path without noticing him. The glimpse he had of his craggy face tickled his memory.

A dock man?

One of the temporary airship workers that bounced between ports?

Security would be on their rounds.

Joe tipped his pocket watch out of the breast pocket of his vest, noting the time. This section of the ship was in the midst of a patrol gap.

The man slowed, turning his head as though listening for sounds behind him.

On instinct, Joe ducked back into the alcove of a service door.

The way the man carried himself and his surreptitious behavior prickled Joe's instincts.

Thief?

Another thief after his father's property?

As soon as the man resumed his pace, Joseph followed with quick, soundless strides, casting glances up and down the hallway lest anyone notice him following this curiosity.

Joe watched as the man inspected the lock securing the cargo hold.

What is he after?

A thief could be after Joe's father's property, or that of anyone else on the ship. Nearly everyone aboard was wealthy.

A guard approached from the opposite direction. "Feeding time?"

The man spun toward the guard. "Uhm, yes sir."

"Where are the dishes? Be quick."

"Here," the man pulled a wrapped lump from his pocket. "I forgot the water, but I can give it this."

The guard unlocked the door and the man slipped inside.

"You, security," a woman's voice called. "My mistress has need of you.

Joe risked a glance.

The guard's body blocked the sight of the woman as he slid the door closed. "Who is your mistress?"

"Baroness Von Schlieffen. One of the ship's servants absconded with one of her possessions."

"Again? I'll find Mr. Jones for you." He followed her away.

Joe crept toward the cargo room.

He glanced up and down the narrow corridor as he listened at the door, hand on the latch, waiting several moments before easing the door open. He strained to hear the inaudible murmur of voices over the steady sound of the ship's engine.

An accomplice?

His hand brushed over his hidden weapons, ensuring they were in place.

A muffled scream ignited his instincts.

In seconds, he was through the door, moving to restrain the man from grappling with a smaller individual next to the gaping bay door.

The larger man slammed the smaller figure against the frame of the open door.

Leveraging his element of surprise, Joe yanked the smaller figure back toward the interior of the room, then quickly overpowered and subdued the man he'd been following.

"Summon security," he ordered with a glance, and did a double take over the sounds of hissing and growling as a caged tiger cub pawed at its bars. The smaller victim slumped next to the cage.

Hell's balls!

"Lin Mei?"

Now his opponent dove forward, trying to regain the advantage, until Joe pulled his pistol from its concealed holster and pointed it at the man's forehead. "Hold still, before you no longer have a choice," he barked, shoving the exterior door closed and dropping the bar back into place.

Sparing Lin Mei another glance, he assessed her state and realized she was in poor health and needed further assistance.

The ship's engines droned on around them.

"You won't use that in this ship," the man said to Joe in heavily accented English.

"Won't I?" Joe growled back. He cocked the hammer. "I don't miss, and the airship is built to handle most anything."

With the pistol trained on Lin Mei's assailant, Joe moved back toward the interior door, pulling it open. He stepped out and called for security. Two men came running up the narrow corridor immediately.

"We also need a physician," Joe said to one man, who nodded.

As soon as they took Lin Mei's attacker into custody, Joe rushed to her side, where she remained collapsed next to the angry little white tiger cub.

He carefully pressed his fingers to the pulse point of her delicate throat and checked her breathing.

What the hell is she doing here?

He adjusted her posture so that she was no longer slumped face down over a crate. Sweeping his hands over her body, then up her neck and scalp he found a bleeding gash on the back of her head.

Joe briefly turned his curiosity to the cub, trying to claw him through the bars.

White with blue eyes, it swiped at him with extended claws. "You'll be alright, just calm yourself," he said, voice soft.

Its ears twitched as it stared at him, hovering over Lin Mei.

Returning his attention to his best friend's sister, he gently brushed aside the hair tangled over her face. Without thinking, he pressed his lips to her forehead. "Lin Mei?"

Heart in his throat, he stroked his hands along the sides of her face, attempting to rouse her. On closer inspection, he noticed how lackluster her hair and skin appeared. The pallor of her face and the sharpness of her cheekbones alarmed him. Then he noticed several rends and tears of her clothing, revealing healed-over scrapes and gashes.

"What the hell is going on here?" he growled.

Rather than continue to wait for the ship's physician to arrive, Joe picked Lin Mei up from the floor and carried her out of the cargo hold toward his own quarters, careful to avoid any curious on-lookers. The cub's howls and cries trailed after him.

Instinct forced discretion.

Security had seen her, and they would report her presence to Jones.

Joe carried Lin Mei's petite form cradled in his arms. Awkwardly releasing the latch to his room, he kicked it closed and strode the few paces to his bunk.

Easing her slight frame onto the mattress, he tenderly ensured her head rested on his pillow before he left her momentarily to retrieve an extra blanket.

Stepping back, he studied her face as his mind raced. His gut sank as he considered all of the scenarios leading to her presence and state in the cargo hold.

He gulped down the dread.

Andrew will be frantic with worry.

Joe's heart pounded with indecision. He didn't want to leave her alone, but she needed a physician.

The instant he realized he was pacing, he ceased and stepped out of his room to search for the physician himself.

He wasn't in his office or in the tiny examination room. Continuing his search, he paused at the open doors of the lounge, scanning it for the man he sought.

Delilah Winter's alert face passed through his line of sight in his quest. Ignoring her, he strode toward the dining hall, hoping to find him there.

He made one final check with Jones in case the physician had gone to cargo hold as requested.

He must be in private quarters with a patient.

Joe spun on his heel, heading straight back to his own room, hoping Lin Mei would awaken to tell him how in the hell she ended up in the cargo hold.

By the time he reached for the latch to his door, he wasn't sure what kind of explanation he was hoping for, but sure that no matter what it was, it wouldn't be good.

However, he wasn't expecting to find Lin Mei staring at him, wide-eyed and ready to bolt when he opened the door.

CHAPTER ELEVEN

❖─◆◗❂◖◆─❖

LIN MEI'S EYES POPPED open. She lurched into a sitting position and gripped her head as it swam. Her surroundings blurred as she attempted to orient herself.

Not the cargo hold.

The ship's engine continued to drone. She was on a narrow bed in a simple room. She blinked her eyes, forcing them to focus despite the pain and pressure behind them.

A valise, gentleman's hat, walking stick and overcoat hung from a rack in the corner. The scent lingering in the room was familiar. A shaving kit sat on a small table next to the washbasin.

A man's room.

Ming!

Pushing the blanket aside, she swung her feet to the floor and took a breath before attempting to stand.

She dropped back onto the mattress, her head spinning harder. The back of it ached as moisture leaked down her nape.

What happened? The man from the dock... the gaping door over the ocean... pain as her head struck the wall, and ... Professor Kaisin?

That can't be right.

Rushed footsteps drew her attention to the door just as it flew open. Joseph Kaisin's form filled the frame. His expression triggered her fight-or-flight instincts.

Lin Mei blinked in confusion.

She still couldn't know if Ming's cage belonged to him or not. If he was responsible for her fate. If the men trying to hurt her worked for him.

Her head hurt too much. She was too tired and hungry to think things through properly.

All she knew was that she'd been attacked, and Ming was now alone.

"What's going on, Joe?" A woman's voice sounded from behind him, distracting him for a second.

Lin Mei bolted, attempting to squeeze through the narrow space between Joseph Kaisin's waist and the door frame.

With lightning reflexes, his hand closed over her arm above the elbow, and he spun her back into the room. A second later, she found herself back on the bed, staring up at him and a woman she'd never seen before.

Both wore stern expressions as they stared down at her.

"Joe?" the woman asked, scowling at Lin Mei as she repeated her earlier question. "What's going on?"

"I don't know yet. This is Lin Mei Lau."

"Lau?" The woman's brows rose, changing her expression. "As in *our* Lau? Surely not, Joe. And in *your* room?"

"Unfortunately, yes. Our Lau. And it's not what you're thinking. Look more closely at her, Winter. She needs a physician. I just found her under attack in the cargo hold."

"Bollocks."

"Indeed."

"You'll have to wire Andrew as soon as we dock at Singapore."

"I will."

Lin Mei blinked as the two stared at her but spoke to one another like she wasn't listening.

"She looks like she needs a pot of tea, and half a dozen scones," the woman said, her expression turned assessing. Her nose wrinkled. "And a bath."

Bath?

Heat crept up Lin Mei's neck, infusing her face.

"She needs the physician, but he's otherwise engaged."

"Hmm, yes." The woman stepped closer, peering at Lin Mei's forehead. "Would you care to come to my room, Ms. Lau? If you're able to walk, I can help you clean up."

"I'm not going anywhere with either of you," she blurted, heart pounding, confused and unsure of what they intended. Perhaps they would complete what the other unknown assailants had tried. "Who are you?"

The woman straightened and backed up a step. "Just a friend of the professor's. Looks as though you've offended her, Joe. What have you done now?"

Professor Kaisin raised a brow as he turned his scowl to the woman now.

"How the devil should I know? Last I saw her was at dinner with Andrew before final checks for my father's cargo prior to departure."

"How could you?" Lin Mei burst out again.

After days of being locked in the dark room with only Ming for company and the constant fear for her life, Lin Mei was at her brink.

"Pardon me, madam?" Professor Kaisin barked as he stared at her, aghast. "How could I what?"

"Oh dear god, Joseph, please tell me you didn't seduce Andrew Lau's little sister? You've got to stop leaving broken hearts in your wake, Joe." The woman laughed. "He will mangle you."

"What? No! Don't be ridiculous, Winter."

They were joking when Lin Mei's emotions and world were swirling and tumbling. Her head continued to spin faster and harder the more upset she became. "How could you cage Ming like that? Does Andrew know you and your father experiment on babies?"

Professor Kaisin gaped at her. "We would do no such thing."

"What do you mean?" the woman, Winter, demanded, leaning toward her, hands on hips.

Lin Mei pressed her lips together, stopping any words that could endanger Ming further.

"What babies?" Professor Kaisin demanded, stepping forward. "Where could you possibly get such a ludicrous idea as that?"

Lin Mei struggled for words to amend her outburst. "Animal babies."

"Animal babies?" Winter demanded. "Regular ones or of a specific color?"

"What the devil does it matter, Delilah? Ms. Lau is clearly distressed and in need of medical care. Why else would she say such strange things?"

Winter glanced behind her, then turned to lock the door. She approached Lin Mei, crouching before her. When she spoke, her voice lost all the sharpness that shaped it before. "Ms. Lau, please tell me about these animals."

"Winter, I don't—,"

"Hush Joe," she shot over her shoulder, then searched Lin Mei's face, her expression soft and open, inviting her to share her secret.

But the way the woman looked at Lin Mei, pleading for her to give her information that Lin Mei knew would expose Ming.

On the cusp of sharing her secret with these two people she really knew nothing about, Lin Mei instead whispered, "I-I'm so very ill."

Ms. Winter's expression shuttered with disappointment, but the scowl didn't return. Instead, she seemed... concerned.

A sharp knock at the door drew everyone's attention as a muffled voice sounded through the thin barrier. "Professor Kaisin, you called for a physician? How may I help you?"

Lin Mei jerked back away from the voice, heart racing.

Professor Kaisin gave her the impression he didn't know what she spoke of.

Can I trust him?

She stared up into his blue eyes.

The concern in his expression caused her heart to flutter, loosening the knot of fear. It was hard to ignore how handsome he was, despite knowing all too well she could still be in danger.

Pressing her lips against the girlish emotions, she reached for logic.

Memories from just a short time ago flooded her. Professor Kaisin and her brother's easy time together. And given Andrew's distrustful nature, that said a lot about the professor.

There was no more time to decide as he turned to admit the doctor.

"I will come back later, Joe. I have some things to look into," Ms. Winter said, glancing at Lin Mei, then departed ahead of the physician entering the room.

Arms crossed, the professor hovered by the door while the physician tended to Lin Mei.

Expressionless, the older man inspected her as though he were tending livestock. He spoke only to instruct her so that he could provide an assessment, which he reported to Professor Kaisin before leaving the room.

"Aside from several healed over wounds, and a few newer ones, including a hard knock on her head, your...ehm, servant is dehydrated. Broth and porridge for a few days should suit her fine to regain her strength and return to her duties."

"The lady is not my servant. She's the sister of a good friend of mine."

"No need to dissemble, sir. I assure you I am discreet."

Professor Kaisin's scowl returned as he stared at the man.

Lin Mei's cheeks flamed.

"Send me the invoice tomorrow. Good evening, sir." Professor Kaisin opened the door for the older man, who gave him a curt bow and left.

From the open door, Professor Kaisin caught the attention of a passing ship's servant and requested that food be brought to his room.

Closing the door, he turned his blue gaze on Lin Mei. When he spoke, his tone brooked no further argument. "Now, Ms. Lau, you will tell me what the devil has happened."

She swallowed, gauging what to do next.

CHAPTER TWELVE

❖

JOE REMOVED HIS JACKET, placed it on its stand in the corner, and loosened his cravat while he waited for Ms. Lau to tell him what the bloody hell was going on.

What he really wanted to be doing was aggressively interrogating the cargo thief to determine what exactly he'd done to her.

Very aggressively.

Andrew is going to go mad.

He paused a moment to study her again.

His throat tightened as he struggled to keep his emotions in check, assessing her bruised face and ragged clothing.

So delicate. Like a butterfly.

Butterfly.

Lin Mei—soft, kind, bright eyes and quick smile.

Gone.

Brittle, closed, wary, withdrawn.

During the doctor's inspection, she seemed to calm, but the distrust that remained in her eyes twisted Joe's heart.

"Your brother is most probably losing his mind right now. And your mother, of course."

He had to know what had happened. He didn't want to, but he had to.

The leather of his gloved hands creaked as they curled into fists.

She visibly swallowed, her dark eyes darting toward the door like she was planning to bolt again.

He sighed, recalling the goon in the cargo room, and forced himself to relax.

The butterfly had a wounded wing.

"I won't hurt you, Lin Mei. I'm going to do everything I can to help you return home to your family and catch whoever caused this situation.

She visibly relaxed—another fraction—but remained tense. Her gaze returned to the door.

He pulled the room's only chair over so that he'd be at her level and still block her path to the door.

"Let's begin with how you got onto the ship," he suggested as he sat, resting both forearms on his knees, leaning closer.

Don't reach for her.

She considered him for an eternal moment.

He linked his fingers together, waiting.

The set of her shoulders eased. She breathed deeper as she searched his face.

Coming to some decision, curiosity sparked in her eyes now. "Professor Kaisin, are antiquities professors usually adept at catching villains?" The corner of her mouth twitched as her gaze became more astute.

The question took him off guard, as did the change in her disposition.

His butterfly wasn't completely gone.

"In general, no, I suppose not. But I shall do my best." He noted with some relief that her fear of *him* subsided. "And you are safe here, Ms. Lau. I assure you."

She nodded, then caught her lower lip between her teeth as she considered her words. "If I tell you what happened, you must promise me that you won't tell Andrew anything alarming and you won't ship me back from the next port."

Joe froze, studying her closely, alarm bells ringing in his head.

What in hellfire has she gotten herself into?

"I'll make no promises of the sort."

"I thought you said I could trust you, Joe?"

He swallowed, hearing his name on her lips.

"I did. You know Andrew would try to flay me if he even suspected I kept secrets from him regarding your safety, Ms. Lau."

"You're afraid of my brother?"

Joe took a moment to control his answer. "No."

It was curious how much her proximity unsettled him.

She frowned at him, then lifted her chin and said, "The man who attacked me is also one of them men who abducted me."

Joe gaped at her.

"He had orders to question me and throw me out of the cargo hold into the ocean before we reached Singapore." Her chin inched up another notch.

He sucked in a breath, nearly lost by the defiance in her eyes.

It didn't matter how disheveled she was.

By the gods, she was beautiful. And feisty.

Damnation.

"Again, why? Why the blazes would anyone want to throw you off the ship?"

"The same reason they abducted me! To hide their nefarious activities."

Joe's mouth snapped shut.

'How could you cage Ming like that? Does Andrew know you and your father experiment on babies?'

"Who is Ming?"

Ms. Lau jerked away from him. "No one."

"You accused me of caging Ming. Who is that?"

...animal babies...

"Is Ming the tiger cub?"

Ms. Lau's eyes widened, darting toward the door again when there was a knock.

"A moment," Joe said, with a glance at her tense face.

He opened the door. A servant waited on the other side with a tray. He stood aside to allow her access to complete her job, remaining vigilant.

Anything could happen. And from what Ms. Lau had already confessed, it would seem much already had.

The servant deposited the tray of food on the small table close to the bunk, curtsied with eyes downcast, and departed without further incident.

Joe lifted the lid from the dishes and peered into their contents. With a nod, he set the lid aside and reclaimed his chair across from Ms. Lau.

"Tell me what happened while you eat. Please, from the start. How did you come to be in the cargo hold?"

Her gaze turned feral as she stared at the food before snatching a bowl and a spoon from the tray and shoveled congee into her mouth. She stopped after several mouthfuls and gasped for breath, eyes closed as she swallowed and dug into the bowl again. Before she'd eaten half of its contents, she dropped it back on the tray and snatched a bowl of broth up and drank it down.

"When was the last time you ate?"

"Tea house." She gasped between gulps.

Tea house? He blinked. The realization slugged him like an iron mallet. He swallowed.

How many days ago? A week?

He shook his head. Not possible. How is she alive?

"You may want to take it slow, otherwise you'll make yourself sick."

She nodded, staring into the bowl clutched between her palms. She set it down and slid the tray toward the wall behind her, away from Joe.

"I won't take it from you, but if you're hungry later, we can order more—freshly made."

She shook her head. "It isn't for me. It's for Mi—the cub in the cage."

She drew in a deep breath and eased it out between her teeth, studying him. "I will tell you, but I promise you, Andrew will be quite upset if you tell him what I'm about to say."

And she did.

The accusation of spying for the constabulary or the crown, the abduction and overheard orders. The attack and defense of her life.

He recalled the image of her struggling with the much larger assailant next to the open door.

His jaw tightened.

When Joe had entered the cargo room, she was seconds from being thrown out of it.

If he hadn't intervened...

"But, why didn't you just alert security to your presence? They would have taken care of you right away. Every crewman aboard this ship knows your brother. Surely you understand that even if I abstain from relaying your story to him, anyone else aboard this ship very likely will alert him to your presence. Including the Captain."

"That's why I need you to promise you won't send me back."

"Why not?"

"I can't leave—I can't go. Not yet."

"Surely you're not abandoning your family and risking your safety because you think a cub might be lonely?"

"Lonely, yes, but also terrified. She's endangered," Lin Mei snapped at him, her fear gone now. "Those people, whoever they are, are going to experiment on her."

Joe sighed. "As appalling as that may be, there is little anyone can do about that, Lin Mei."

She jumped to her feet, causing the dishes to rattle. "I won't have it." Her cheeks took on a heated hue and her eyes glittered as she regarded him. "And if you try to stop me from protecting her, I'll... I'll tell everyone you compromised me." Her hands swept down her ragged clothing.

Joe was on his feet as indignation swept through him, "Hey now, I—,"

"Yes, and Andrew will take that piece of news very well, won't he?"

Joe gulped as he stared at Ms. Lau.

Yes, the delicate butterfly he envisioned her to be, had just morphed into a feral tigress with teeth bared, determined to protect her adopted young.

Now he saw the real resemblance between the Lau siblings.

There were few men that Joe was reluctant to cross and even fewer that he feared.

He and Andrew had trained together. They were evenly matched in skill and self-control. But if it came down to it, there were very few things that would cause his oldest friend to rampage. And this accusation would be one of them. Joe respected Andrew, but he also knew that Andrew would take one look at his little sister and resolve to destroy anyone that hurt her.

Joe squeezed his gloved mechanical hand into a fist. This wouldn't end well. Not well at all.

"And if I agree to allow this blackmail?"

"Then I will sing your praises about how you rescued me and kept me safe from further attempts on my life all the way to London. Like the perfect gentleman that you are."

He paused at this, finally making further connections.

Whomever the caged cub belonged to, they didn't want any witnesses, initially thinking she was a spy. They were willing to dispose of Ms. Lau in order to keep their activities quiet.

Why?

He studied her a moment as she continued to stare at him, waiting for his further response.

She'd endured much, and risked her life to protect this tiger cub.

Again, why?

He removed his glasses, pinching the bridge of his nose.

Joe drew a deep, deep breath, realizing right then and there that he was in a lot of trouble, as his heart skittered at the sight of her magnificent determination.

She was going to need a protector.

And protecting was Joe's best job.

Replacing his glasses, he held her direct gaze.

Joe squeezed his mechanical hand.

He'd let Delilah down. He wouldn't let Lin Mei down, too.

I can't.

Because, as he drank in her fierce expression, he knew it would destroy him if he did.

"Alright, Ms. Lau. I will help you."

CHAPTER THIRTEEN

⸻◈❈◈⸻

LIN MEI SCOWLED AT the Professor.

He'd forced her to go to Mr. Jones' office.

'Before the entire security team pulls the ship apart looking for you.'

Kaisin ignored her angry glare, opting to stare at the wall behind Mr. Jones' desk.

Jones regarded her with genuine concern.

"Ms. Lau, I missed making your acquaintance during your visit with Constable Lau before departure." Jones bowed his head to her before retaking the place behind his desk. "And I am deeply concerned with the revelation of your abduction and detainment in our cargo room. I apologize for the necessity to ask you to recount your ordeal so that I may submit a full report to the ship's captain and for the local constabulary back in Hong Kong."

With a final glance at Joe, Lin Mei cleared her throat. "Professor Kaisin assured me I could remain aboard the Soaring Dragon—under his protection—until Andrew could collect me in London."

Mr. Jones raised one eyebrow as his gaze flicked to Joe. "Professor?"

There was some non-verbal exchange between the two that Lin Mei couldn't fathom. When she turned to look up at Joe's face, he gave Jones a sharp nod.

By now, both of Jones' brows were up as he blew out a breath. "And you will communicate with Constable Lau on the matter."

Joe adjusted his glasses. "Of course. I take full responsibility."

Jones averted his gaze, shuffling report papers from one side of his desk to the other, muttering, "It's your head, mate."

"It is. You know Lau and I are old friends."

Jones' gaze flicked back up to Joe as another meaningful exchange occurred that Lin Mei couldn't read.

She scowled at both of them now. "I have one request, if I may."

Jones leaned back in his seat and clasped his hands together on his desk. "How may I be of service, Ms. Lau?"

"I'd like permission to visit Ming each day."

"Ming?"

"The tiger cub," Joe said.

Jones' eyebrows disappeared into his hairline. "The tig—you want to go back into the cargo room where you were held prisoner so you can visit the tiger cub?"

"Yes." Lin Mei swallowed, shooting Joe a furtive glance.

Lin Mei's impatience built as the man slid his gaze to Joe again.

Joe shrugged.

"It isn't as though I'm going to take anything. Sir." She snapped her lips together before she said anything else that might hurt her case. "We bonded. And she likes me."

"I'll think on the matter, Ms. Lau. My men are very busy and wouldn't be able to take time away from their duties to shadow you."

"The man that attacked me is in your custody, isn't he, sir?"

"He is."

"I should be safe enough."

"We don't know that. He hasn't been questioned yet," Joe said.

The sound of leather creaking drew both Lin Mei's and Mr. Jones' attention to the professor's gloved fists.

Jones' lips compressed into a stern line. "He's right, Ms. Lau. We must investigate this serious matter. Only then will I think about allowing you access to the cargo room."

She opened her mouth to protest, but Jones cut her off.

"That investigation begins with your statement, Ms. Lau. The sooner we get started, the sooner I'll consider your request."

She sighed in defeat but nodded her head, beginning the story anew.

She told them everything. Everything but the facts that Ming changed into a human child, and that she healed her wounds by licking the blood away.

Lin Mei still wasn't sure they wouldn't lock her up, so she decided that part was best left untold.

SEVERAL DAYS AFTER LIN Mei's rescue, the staff corridors were still being heavily monitored.

Delilah Winter recalled Lin Mei Lau's words as she moved through the ship.

She'd not been able to get close to the cargo hold with servants and security hovering near as they interrogated the man who'd attacked Andrew's little sister.

What a curious situation.

She couldn't blame the young woman for her distrust. Delilah understood it all too well. Fighting for your life against an opponent clearly twice your size did much to frazzle your trust in the world.

Having been in Ms. Lau's shoes on more than one occasion, it was one of the reasons Delilah had joined the Queen's service where she'd learned how to defend herself effectively. Quite effectively.

She shoved her wayward thoughts aside as she moved along the corridor, circling back toward the cargo hold, maintaining the air of a lady intent on exercise.

"Damnation," she growled when she rounded the corner and saw the security staff still present. She had to let them do their jobs, but she also needed to confirm her suspicions.

You're slipping, Delilah. You should have planted those devices long before now.

But she'd been so busy trying to cover every other suspect under her surveillance, she'd neglected the one place that, in the end, mattered most.

A thrill rippled through her.

"I know I'm right," she murmured, taking quick stock of the security crew on her approach.

One stepped forward, blocking her path, and nodded in the direction she'd come from. "This corridor is off limits to guests."

Delilah snapped her fan open, fluttering it. "Just seeking a little exercise. I do dislike such confining spaces as a dirigible."

The impertinent servant raised a brow but didn't budge.

"There were whispers of an exotic animal aboard the ship. I'd hoped to get a glance to ease my ennui." She leaned toward him conspiratorially. "Surely, just a little peek wouldn't hurt anyone."

Still, he didn't move beyond a breath and a blink.

She snapped her fan, passing it coyly across the lower half of her face. "Or perhaps *you* could alleviate my boredom." She slid her gaze purposefully up his person, lingering on his broad shoulders before settling boldly on his face.

Crimson crept up his throat and cheeks at an alarming rate as though he'd been scalded by a too-hot tea pot. He cleared his throat and nodded behind her. "Madame, the passenger lounge is that way and up the stairs."

She sighed.

No matter. She could still get what she wanted. It would just be a little more... involved than gaining simple admittance.

"You're right, we've only just met. Perhaps tomorrow evening, then?" She brushed the edge of her fan along his bicep, intent on flustering him further as she turned back toward the lounge, already plotting her next move.

Before reaching the end of the corridor and the stairs that led up to the guest deck, she went around the corner. A glance in each direction confirmed she was alone. Ducking into an unlocked linen storeroom, she peeled her dress off, removed several layers of crinoline and tucked them behind a pile of fluffy white towels.

Turning the dress inside out to expose its plain inner lining, she put it back on, then grabbed a spare apron and cap from a cluster hung on a peg. Listening for sounds outside the door, she looped the apron over her head, tied it behind her waist, and tucked her curls up into the cap.

She'd already done this a couple of times since the beginning of the journey and had a fair assessment of the layout.

Striding past the engine room, she ignored most of the doors until she reached the one at the end. With another glance to confirm she was alone, she stepped inside, then closed and locked the door.

Delilah glanced up, assessing the narrow ceiling hatch as she reached for the sturdiest shelf to climb.

Working her way up into the ceiling, she slid along neatly bundled wires lining the airflow vents supplying the guest deck until she reached the support beams which marked the section of the cargo room, where the ceiling comprised of metal grate panels.

She eased her way across the top of the room until she reached the optimal spot to install her first observation device and set it to transmit.

Movement drew her attention toward the cargo room's main door as she was setting up the third penny-sized device over the tiger cage while it slept.

Lin Mei Lau appeared with a tray of food, easing the door closed behind her. Moving toward the cage, she kept her voice low as she spoke in Mandarin.

"I brought you some food, Ming."

Delilah's grasp of Asian languages wasn't as fluid as she preferred, but she knew enough to understand. She switched on her recording device so she could review and decipher them later to ensure her understanding was correct.

The tiger's ears perked as it turned its head toward Lin Mei.

Delilah waited, breath held, willing the animal to reveal itself as a changeling.

As the young woman approached the cage, the tiger leaped to its paws excitedly.

Lin Mei leaned in to slip her arms through the bars to embrace the tiger cub that now frantically licked her face, making her laugh. "It's alright. I'm alright," she said as the tiger sniffed her intently.

"I'm alright," she said again, grasping the tiger's ears so she could place a kiss on the bridge of its nose. "It just took me a little while to convince Mr. Jones to let me in. He tells me you've been misbehaving and it seems you've been terribly noisy since I was rescued."

Delilah swallowed her rising emotions at the display of open affection between Lin Mei and the tiger cub.

"Here, I know you're hungry." Lin Mei placed a few dumplings through the bars of the cage. She stroked the tiger's fur as it devoured the food. "I can't stay in here with you anymore, but I have an idea."

The tiger's ears twitched as it ate the food.

The young woman pulled an object from her clothes and attempted to pick the lock securing the cage.

"I found a small hairpin on the floor," she muttered, still trying to trigger the release. Lin Mei growled, tugging on the lock, and threw up her hands in defeat.

"I'm going to find the key to this cage. Once I do that, I'll figure out a way to get us off this ship at the next port so we can get you back to your family. Then I'll go back to mine." She gently stroked the cub's furry head and ears.

Delilah's heart pounded in excitement.

I'm right, I know it!

The cub's purring was loud enough to reach her, where she remained hidden from their view.

"But we still have to be careful. I don't know who I can trust, and I know you don't want me to tell anyone your secret either. I will do my best to keep you safe, just like you did your best to keep me healthy by healing me when I cut my arm."

Healing? Delilah blinked as her heart pounded even further.

"Ming, I can't fit the bowls through the bars. I need you to change so you can eat this food and stay strong. We need to be strong when we escape. Do you understand?"

No longer purring, the tiger gave a little huff.

Tears gathered in Delilah's eyes as she watched the white tiger cub transform in a magical wavering mist into a little girl kneeling inside the iron barred cage.

Lin Mei scooped congee from the bowl and eased the spoon between the bars so the child could eat the food.

Delilah struggled to control her emotions for entirely different reasons this time. Her diligence paid off. She was on the right trail.

Now she just needed to know who owned that cage.

She continued to watch Lin Mei and the child until the meal ended, with the child reverting back to her animal form as the young woman left.

Delilah set the last device to transmit, then continued on in the close confines of the ceiling until she reached the room where the captured goon was being interrogated.

By the time she eased herself into position over the office where the goon was held, it seemed that whatever current interrogation was in progress, was over.

Only two figures occupied the small office.

She wasn't surprised to see Joe Kaisin in there, with the exception that he risked breaking his cover. No doubt, he used the excuse that he was connected to Andrew Lau to gain entrance.

However, what did surprise her was the sight of his left hand as he replaced his leather gloves.

Damnation.

I thought I'd taken the brunt of the injuries during the New York mission. I knew the wounds to his hand were bad, just not that bad.

She waited as he left the room. No one else came in. The goon remained tied to a chair; expression terrified.

Delilah smirked. *Ah Joe.*

With a shake of her head, she set more listening devices and returned to her own room, via the closet where she had hidden her things, to re-evaluate her plan.

There was much to do, but she had the confirmation she needed.

Delilah bit her lip as she considered Joe Kaisin and whether she needed him for her mission.

She thought of the New York debacle.

No, Joe wouldn't let another New York happen. But still... her fingers trailed over the left side of her chest.

Not yet.

CHAPTER
FOURTEEN

JOE STEPPED THROUGH THE door of the small office and closed it behind him.

Jones waited outside.

It had taken some negotiation to convince Jones to hold off on his plan to notify Andrew of Lin Mei's presence and predicament by carrier pigeon, rather than by wire at Singapore's port, which resulted in raising his suspicions regarding Joe's intentions toward the young woman.

He leveled his attention at the room's other occupant.

The goon that attacked Lin Mei was bound to a chair, staring back at Joe insolently.

Joe assessed the man, who assessed him back with a lazy smirk.

Images of the man roughly treating Ms. Lau charged to the forefront of his thoughts, distracting from his cool approach.

His fingers curled into fists as he collected his thoughts and re-assumed his professor persona, pacing before the rough goon.

"Do you know who I am?"

The man shrugged.

"My name is Joseph Kaisin. My father is Toussaint Kaisin, a well-known inventor."

The man lifted a brow.

Joe carried on. "I assume you were in the cargo hold to steal some of my father's property, in which pursuit I also assume you failed when the young lady stowaway surprised your efforts."

The man frowned, eyes darting side to side, trying to connect the assumptions Joe offered him.

"I am part of the ship's crew."

"Mr. Jones does not have your identity papers or your contract. Which Hong Kong gang are you working for?"

The man jerked back, startled by the question. "I found a stowaway, as you say, and tried to apprehend her."

"I think I will notify the Hong Kong newspapers that one of the... *Hei Shi* gang members has been apprehended for attempted kidnap and murder of the innocent younger sister of a police constable. A member who gave up his boss under duress."

The man snorted.

Joe tapped a finger on his lips. "Not the *Hei Shi* gang. The *Guan Yu*, then?"

The man's lips compressed as his eyes narrowed on Joe.

Ah, here we go.

"The newspapers would seize the chance to report on the apprehension of a gang member connected to various burglaries in the city while attempting to abscond with my father's property. A big story, indeed."

The man scowled, but still said nothing.

"Why does your boss want my father's property? Resale?" Joe continued his pacing again. "I shouldn't think a gang boss would have any direct interest in an old man's inventions when he has his plate full of organized crime. No, I think his plan is to sell to someone else."

Joe turned his attention back to the goon and his continued silent defiance.

"I'm right, aren't I?" Joe grinned, stepping closer. "Who?"

"Who what?" the goon said with his heavily accented English.

"Who is your boss's buyer? And which of my father's patents is he after?"

"Why should I speak to you? Foreigner. You're all the same."

Joe nodded as though he considered the question as he strode the small space before the goon's chair.

"Well, sir, here is the thing." Joe tugged at the fingers of his leather gloves to remove them. First the right, drawing the goon's attention in the space between his words. Then the left, revealing a mechanical hand.

The goon's eyes widened at the sight of Joe's prosthetic hand as he flexed the fingers.

"Brilliant, isn't it?" Joe said, drawing the man's attention from his hand to his face.

The man's expression registered awe and uncertainty.

"My father made it for me after I lost my natural limb in an... ehm, accident. Very durable. Very solid." He picked up a carved mahogany paper weight, crushing it between his fingers so that it cracked like a gunshot in the small room. "Isn't it impressive? Doesn't require much force at all." Joe looked directly into the man's eyes as a few tiny slivers sprinkled to the floor.

He went on. "That young lady you attacked is the younger sister of a very good friend of mine. Since he isn't here to thrash you himself. I'm feeling somewhat obligated to do it on his behalf."

He curled his fingers into a fist and slowly uncurled them again.

"But I also want to know who your boss's buyer is and what they want. So, I have two very personal, reasons to thrash you."

The man swallowed; eyes fixed on the metal hand. "I won't tell you anything."

"Don't worry. While I know the constabulary in Hong Kong want to put your boss in prison, I'm not asking you to betray him. I just want to know about the foreigner." Joe gambled, homing in on the man's earlier words.

Joe leaned toward the man and tapped his knee with the tip of his index finger of his left hand. The metal made a dull thunking sound as it struck the bone.

The man winced.

"You aren't man enough to do anything to me." The goon finally spat at Joe.

True, the crown frowned on aggressive interrogation. Although that didn't always deter Joe when the circumstances required it. He wouldn't be able to explain this to Jones and word would spread.

Still, he pressed on.

Joe grinned wickedly at him as he adjusted his false spectacles. "Just because I'm a man of learning, doesn't mean I don't have a buried wicked streak."

The goon leaned away from Joe's prosthetic hand reaching for his bobbing Adam's apple.

"Don't all men have some darkness in them?" he flicked his gaze up to the man's eyes. "Some more than others, I'd say."

The man flinched as the cool metal grazed his throat. "You don't scare me." His voice lost its insolence and confidence.

Joe straightened and reached for the already cracked paper weight. Gripping it in his left hand, he crushed it to splinters, maintaining a facade of indifference as he stared at the goon.

Sweat beaded the man's forehead as his eyes darted between the destroyed object and Joe's face.

Interesting.

"Your boss must be a very powerful man to have earned such unwavering loyalty." Joe said.

The man swallowed, gaze finally glued to Joe's metal hand, fear drawing on his features.

Instinct and experience told Joe the goon wouldn't talk. But he'd gleaned enough from him to get an idea of what he was dealing with. There were other ways.

Unable to resist increasing the man's discomfort, he said. "I'll give you time to think about our discussion. Perhaps revisiting the cargo's outdoor hatch might persuade you to help things along."

The man's eyes widened further; a dribble of perspiration slid down his temple.

Joe snapped his leather gloves against his hand before pulling the right one on, flexed his fingers, then pulled the left on and did the same.

"Teatime now. We can chat again after dinner." Joe smiled and left the room.

CHAPTER FIFTEEN

LIN MEI'S MIND RACED with all the scenarios she could imagine about finding the key to Ming's cage. She headed toward Professor Kaisin's room, where he'd insisted she remained until he was assured of her safety.

For days now, her thoughts had been in turmoil.

Ming.

Her family.

Joe.

In Singapore, they'd sent the wire to Hong Kong informing Andrew that she was safe.

She bit her lip. Guilt pounded through her as she recalled Professor Kaisin's words about her family and their worry for her. She hadn't done any of this on purpose, but now that she was here, Lin Mei had to do something to help Ming.

Ming was just a child, like Lin Mei's own little siblings, and she couldn't imagine how she would feel if one of them were stolen like Ming had been.

He's right, Andrew will be very upset and unreasonable.

Even if she was safe.

Safe for now...

The thought trailed away as visceral recollections of her attack froze her in place for a moment. And what would lie ahead for her and Ming once they escaped the ship? Getting the little one home - wherever that was, wouldn't be easy.

Impossible?

Can I do this? Alone?

She wasn't so sure, but there wasn't much choice.

I won't abandon her.

Lin Mei squared her shoulders, increasing her stride.

First, she needed to discover who the cage belonged to.

She'd already searched Professor Kaisin's room for any keys and found none. But that didn't mean he didn't have it on his person.

She'd finally acknowledged that she didn't really think it was his or his father's. Though Lin Mei still didn't believe she could fully trust him with Ming's secret.

He wouldn't believe it, anyway.

He'd just send me home at the very next port, and I can't abandon Ming. I won't.

That woman...Ms. Winter? She had seemed far too interested in what Lin Mei had to say about Ming.

Lin Mei bit her lip.

Ms. Winter knows something.

How much? Would she help? Or is she the same woman that gave the order to speed up my demise?

"Ms. Lau, you should be resting."

She spun at the sharp tone of Professor Kaisin's voice.

Joe.

The glitter in his eyes drew her attention. The intensity and determination brightened the blue depths, stealing her breath as she studied him in the seconds it took him to reach her.

"After being trapped in the cargo room, you wish me to remain confined to your even smaller guest room?"

The set of his wide shoulders eased a fraction as he looked down into her face. "For your safety, yes. Besides, what were you doing back here, of all places?" He glanced up and down the corridor. A servant passed at the junction behind them going in one direction, a porter passed traveling in the opposite. "I'm surprised no one stopped you."

Lin Mei glanced down at her clothes. "I suppose I blend in with the staff. I was just visiting Ming."

Since her rescue, she'd washed and mended her clothing. Unable to scrub out the residual blood stains, she made do.

He considered her. "I don't suppose Ms. Curren's clothes would fit you."

Lin Mei shook her head with a smile. "She's much taller and..." she was going to comment on Ms. Curren's womanly assets but stopped before she could embarrass herself.

"Right. Shall we?" Professor Kaisin gestured toward the stairs that led to the guest quarters. "I will inquire about the availability of her clothing for your use. Perhaps there is something you can alter. We'll have them brought back to my room, where you'll remain. Until we find who your assailant is working with, and your safety is assured."

"You believe someone will attack me again?" Ice swept through her.

Professor Kaisin nodded. "I'm afraid so. We haven't discovered the accomplice you mentioned. You will remain in my room until then."

Lin Mei's foot scuffed the floor.

Joe's hand shot out to steady her.

She gulped, looking up into his intense blue gaze again. Her body flushed from where his hand gently cradled her elbow and spread through her chest, belly and lower as her own gaze swept over him. Too many times, she'd caught herself admiring him. Tall, broad shoulders and thick arms. Young, handsome, strong.

She couldn't deny he made her feel safe and desperately wished she could remember her rescue from the cargo hold.

He carried himself with the same physical confidence that Andrew and his fellow police officers did.

Lin Mei frowned, noting again how he bore no resemblance to any other professor she'd ever seen before.

These last few days had been... challenging.

"That... that would be unwise and—inappropriate, Professor Kaisin. I don't think Andrew would approve, and if anyone from our community should find out, Mama wouldn't be able to secure a marriage match for me."

"Marriage match?" His brow furrowed.

Had he forgotten that she'd mentioned it during their dinner at the tea house?

He has more important things to think about.

"Yes, of course." She paused when she reached the door that led to the stairwell, pulling it open. "As much as I might like to remain unattached and explore the world like Andrew did, my family needs me to make a good match. I'm long overdue, and mother has been patient with me."

"I see." He stepped closer, placing his hand on the door above her head.

Her belly fluttered at his proximity.

She spun to mount the steps. "Mother has several candidates lined up. I just have to choose one, and then the haggling begins." She sighed as she reached the top.

He lingered on the step just below. With his arm stretched out behind her, he was close enough that the warmed scent of his soap drifted toward her.

His frown deepened into a scowl.

"You disapprove?"

The scowl softened as his gaze flickered over her face.

She felt it, like he'd touched her. Every inch of her skin tightened under his stare.

He blinked, straightening. "Only if a match with a local merchant isn't something you want?"

Lin Mei laughed as she turned away. "A merchant! I should be so lucky! Mama would be ecstatic with a match like that. No, my future husband will be a local farmer or a fisherman."

She stopped outside the door to his room with a smile that faltered when she looked up at him.

Solemn, his gaze fixed on her face as his right hand lifted toward her. "That would be such... a waste of your beauty."

His gloved fingers drifted along her cheek.

"Beauty is useless when you have a family to support," she whispered, desperately ignoring the flutter in her belly and the stammer of her heart.

He snatched his hand from her face and cleared his throat. "Right. Absolutely right. And it's certainly none of my business in any regard." He opened the door and gestured for her to precede him. "However, your current safety is. Please wait here while I speak with the ship's concierge regarding Ms. Curren's property. I'm sure as her sister-in-law, you are entitled to their use—given the circumstances."

Shoving aside the disappointment of his retreat, she stepped into the tiny room. "It's no bother, really. If they have spare servant's clothing. In fact, I could bunk with them if they have a spare cot." As an afterthought, she added, "I should work with them to earn my keep while I'm on board."

It would be much easier to explore the ship unnoticed, dressed like a servant.

Then I can get Ming out of here and go back to my family... and an eventual future husband I don't want.

And, put some distance between us before I do something we'll both regret.

Lin Mei clipped that thought and focused on the present.

He lingered in the doorway. "I can't protect you if you're mixed in with the staff and out of sight and reach. Please wait here while I see about Ms. Curren's clothes." He closed the door behind him, leaving her alone.

Alone and surrounded by everything that reminded her that she was in his personal space. She slid her fingers over the shoulder of his dinner jacket hung on the coat rack, the brim of his top hat set on the shelf above, then inspected his shaving equipment.

Not for the first time.

When she lifted the frothing brush, the scent of his soap infiltrated her senses.

Like he had.

She dropped back onto the cot as her thoughts bounced between the dangerous growth of her feelings for him and her determination to see to Ming's safety.

His bed.

Dangerous thoughts, Lin Mei.

Her fingers splayed across the duvet as she slid her hand over the smooth fabric of Professor Kaisin's bed.

Joe's bed.

Lin Mei slept in it, while the gentlemanly professor rested in the uncomfortable chair by the door.

Surely there's enough room for two...

She squeezed her eyes shut against her confused emotions.
Lin Mei! Don't be stupid.

*You just told him you'd be unmarriageable if there was even
a hint of dishonorable conduct here.*

But...would that be so bad?

Her heart tripped as she slipped into her imagination.
What would it feel like to kiss him?

She pictured his beautiful blue eyes.

Her fingertips brushed her lips.

Eyes closed, she allowed the fantasy to play out.

His lips on hers. Warm and gentle?

No.

Another shiver rippled through her.

She sensed the passion buried beneath his *professor* exterior.
It was there when she caught him looking at her.

She sighed.

A kiss from Joe would be nothing like the clumsy kisses
she'd experienced from a few of the local boys.

Boys.

Which Joe was not.

Tall, broad shouldered, handsome, cultured, and educated.

He was a man of the world. A wealthy man. A European
with far more important things to do than mind a worthless
little farm girl until her big brother could come and collect
her.

She allowed the fantasies for just a few moments. Kisses and
more.

Which inevitably would lead to children. They always did.
It could never work... could it?

Even if it could, it would mean leaving. A European aristocrat would never live in a mountain village with her family.

But isn't that what you truly want, Lin Mei? To get away from your tiny little village and travel the world like Andrew does?

She mentally ticked off her arguments.

You barely know him.

You're apparently still in danger.

You're foolish to give your heart to a man that doesn't want it anyway.

Lin Mei put a quick end to the fantasies and returned to her decisive plan to rescue Ming.

She glanced around the small room with a sigh.

If Professor Kaisin continued to look at her the way he did earlier in the corridor, maintaining her resolve would be a challenge.

But I will. Ming's life is far more important than what my heart wants.

She rose from the bed, approaching the looking glass.

I can't abandon her.

She pushed the loose strands of hair from her forehead to inspect the quickly healing bruise. The pain had already receded, as had the angry swelling surrounding the broken skin.

Ming's magic kept me going. I will do the same for her.

CHAPTER SIXTEEN

Bleary-eyed, Joe sipped his coffee, hoping it would give him at least a few good hours of clarity.

He realized his mistake long before morning arrived after that first night.

Lin Mei.

Days later, it was still a mistake.

A colossal one.

He repeatedly reminded himself that he was a gentleman.

It didn't matter that Lin Mei was his oldest friend's younger sister.

He'd somehow lost control over where his thoughts ought to be and where they wanted to go.

Society was nearly apoplectic on the subject of sharing of close quarters with non-relations without a chaperone.

Chaperones were created for a reason, Joe.

A good reason.

Despite his focus on his new self-assigned mission to protect Ms. Lau from harm and return her to the safety of her family, his thoughts, day and night, drifted to her.

He'd loaned her his night shirt and given her space to bathe, mend and wash her clothing.

Just knowing she was undressed and bathing in his room, awakened his baser, usually strictly controlled needs.

The mental image of her wearing nothing but his shirt hadn't helped his plight.

The second night, the staff had replaced his delicate chair with a plusher one from the lounge. It cramped the limited space even further.

He should have slept on the floor. He'd slept on worse while in the field.

From the floor, she wouldn't be in his line of sight all night long.

His training as an agent meant he slept light. Alert to the slightest sounds in proximity.

Which meant every sigh and whisper she made in her sleep, drew his attention to her lovely, golden-hued face, visible in the low light of his room.

The bed linens hushed every time she shifted her body beneath the duvet.

I should have slept on the bloody floor.

He'd resisted thoughts of her since their first meeting.

It had been easier with his focus on preparations for the journey.

Now, all he had to distract himself was his daily tour of the airship to monitor the other passengers.

In his bid to keep her safe, he'd made it his mission to be her shadow.

Fool.

This was going to end in violence between himself and Andrew.

Or it would end in absolute bliss.

The breakfast room's servant appeared with a carafe to refill his cup.

I ought to find Lin Mei somewhere else to sleep.

You can't protect her if she's elsewhere.

The same two thoughts revolved in an endless rotation.

He counted the days until they reached the next port.

And yet, in the middle of the night, he dreaded reaching it as his gaze caressed the smooth contours of her face while she slept.

Like a chant, he repeated thoughts to encourage his focus on her safety. And her virtue.

She was right. If he compromised her, she wouldn't be able to make a good match once she returned home.

We barely know each other.

He stared at the passing clouds through the lounge's tall windows.

I feel like I've always known her.

That day in her village...

Wasn't enough.

He drummed the table as he thought.

What if I keep her?

Would she have me?

Even if she did, then what?

He flexed his left hand, still encased in his leather glove, to keep it hidden from the world.

She isn't anything like Eleanora.

He doubted she would recoil in revulsion at the sight of his unnatural appendage.

But what if she did?

Then you will know.

Why am I even considering this? The idea of a union between Andrew's sister and myself is ludicrous.

The grim reality was that Joe knew deep down, he shouldn't be considering a union between himself and any woman that sought a relationship longer than a few hours.

Not with his line of work.

Crown work.

Joe had applied for a permanent position at the university, to be there for his father, but he still hadn't decided if he was done with agency work for good.

Not yet.

It still called to him.

He glanced down at his left hand.

As an agent of the crown, there was absolutely no security.

Never in one place to make a proper home or develop genuine relationships. Never knowing which mission would be the last.

New York nearly was, for both him and Delilah.

They'd survived. Mostly.

He flexed his hands again, focusing on the sensation of the prosthetic hand his father had made to replace the one he'd lost in the New York blast.

Everything changed.

It was good to see Delilah had moved on and was still in the field.

He'd been lucky that was all he lost. She had lost more.

And they'd both lost their partnership.

That incident had also been the tipping point in his relationship with Eleanora. The counterbalance had sunk to one side, and she'd stepped off on the other.

Joe hadn't seen her since the day of their reunion, he with his freshly installed appendage. The following morning, he received her curt letter informing him of the end of their engagement.

Eleanora's horror at the sight of his mechanical hand was enough. He hadn't needed the letter.

'Any professor of antiquities who was careless enough to lose a hand in a freak accident on a dig wasn't a suitable candidate for

a husband or future father. How could you hold your own child with that?'

It was just as well he hadn't confided in his true work.

Or perhaps he should have. Sooner. Before he ever proposed to her. He'd have spared her a year's worth of time in her hunt for the perfect husband.

Eleanora hadn't left him heartbroken. But she had left him room to rethink his future.

His thoughts flicked back to Ms. Lau.

He sipped more of his bitter black coffee, refreshed and hot on his tongue.

I won't make that mistake again.

Keep her safe with virtue and reputation intact until her family could send for her.

It was the same argument, night after night.

Temptation, reminder, resolve.

He stared at the bottom of his empty cup. Tired.

I'm not going to survive this journey.

CHAPTER
SEVENTEEN

PROFESSOR KAISIN HAD INSISTED on escorting Lin Mei to and from each visit with Ming, resulting in several heated disagreements.

She stood now, tray in hands, jaw clenched as he combed the room for any lurking attackers.

There were none, so he let himself out and left the door open several inches should he need to rush back in.

She rolled her eyes and set the tray next to Ming's cage.

"He's worse than my brother," she whispered to the top of the cub's furry head as she purred and rubbed Lin Mei's face between the bars.

Lin Mei bit her lip. "We are almost to the next port, and I still haven't been able to figure out how to find the key to open this cage." She sighed and rubbed her hands over her face. "But even when I can get you off this ship, how do we get you back to your family? I have no money."

She stroked Ming's fur through the bars as she thought—which was much easier to do when Professor Kaisin, with his gorgeous blue eyes and boyish dimples, wasn't hovering nearby to distract her.

"I should push the idea of earning my keep on board the ship, besides it will give me something to do. And if I can make enough money to buy us passage back from another port, then we're set. Or we just stay on board all the way back again."

Lin Mei frowned. "No, that won't do unless I can hide you somehow. If you would stay in your girl form once we get you out of here, we can pretend you're my little sister or my daughter. You'd be too hard to hide as a tiger."

Ming made a noise and put her chin down on her paws.

Content to just sit and pet Ming for the moment, Lin Mei's eyes drifted to the water bowl in the cage. Someone was checking in on her. Previously, it had been the man posing as crew that had orders to throw Lin Mei overboard. Would another replace him at Ceylon?

She swallowed the sudden rise of panic that question brought her.

"I have to get you out of here," she whispered, stroking Ming's head one last time before she rose to leave. She drew a deep breath, set her shoulders and strode toward the door.

Professor Kaisin waited for her in the narrow corridor. She closed the cargo door, then strode past him toward the security office and knocked on the door.

"What's wrong?" Professor Kaisin asked her.

"Nothing is wrong. I simply wish to speak to Mr. Jones."

The door opened. Jones covered his initial surprise and greeted them. "Good morning, Ms. Lau. Professor Kaisin, how may I help you?"

Lin Mei moved past him to sit on one of the chairs set before his desk.

"Can I get you some tea?" he asked, hesitant.

"No thank you, I won't be long."

Jones sat behind his desk to face Lin Mei.

She glanced back to see Professor Kaisin standing inside the door, frowning at her.

Turning back to Jones, she said, "I wish to work aboard the ship. I can work as service crew during the day and provide some small entertainment during the evening dinner."

Jones' eyebrows lifted as he processed her words.

She rushed on. "I've performed traditional dance at local festivals every year since I was a child. I could do that during the dinner hour, since my sister-in-law is currently unavailable to provide entertainment. Unless, of course, she has been temporarily replaced?"

Jones' gaze flicked to Kaisin behind her before responding cautiously. "No, she hasn't. And we can always use extra servants on the ship. The guests can be quite... demanding. Even I'm run off my feet answering petty spats. You'd be surprised at the controlled chaos that goes on." He gave a short laugh. "Your brother was a master at this job."

"Has there been any further developments with the gang member that attacked Ms. Lau?" Kaisin interjected.

Jones shook his head. "He hasn't said anything at all that would give us any hints as to why he attacked her. Nothing."

"Where is he now?" Lin Mei asked as a wave of fear washed through her.

"Locked away in our brig. We will hand him over to the constabulary when we reach Ceylon."

"That's it? No further investigation?" Lin Mei struggled to keep her voice level.

"As soon as he disembarks this ship and is in their custody, he is no longer our concern. We must allow the justice system its due. We have a rigorous schedule to keep."

"What if another attacker infiltrates the ship at another port?" Kaisin demanded.

Jones sighed. "That could happen. But Ms. Lau has already been exposed aboard the ship and has already had an opportunity to divulge whatever it is they think she knows about their operations."

"They may still be after my father's property."

"Professor Kaisin, we're doing all we can with our limited resources aboard this ship. We're constantly having to answer to petty squabbles. Even when I post someone to stand guard outside the cargo room, I need to pull them away to deal with something else. We are a contained unit here. There is nowhere for anyone to go between ports. Please allow us to do our jobs."

Lin Mei jumped in here. "Please consider my request to work aboard the ship too. I'd like to earn my way since I'm here. I'll pay my way and send the remainder home to my family. I can bunk with the other servants."

"I still have concerns about Ms. Lau's safety." Kaisin insisted.

She turned in her seat to glare at the professor before turning back to Jones. "I appreciate Professor Kaisin's gentlemanly effort to see to my wellbeing, but I cannot in good conscience allow him to continue to sleep on a chair while I have the luxury of his bunk. Especially when he has paid good money to travel aboard the ship and I have not."

"There are no spare bunks to offer. The only room that has remained unoccupied is Ms. Curren's due to the storage of her property for her performances. She's a valuable asset to the Soaring Dragon, as is your brother."

"I can be too. Let me use her room. I will work on the ship."

"I will speak to the captain at the next opportunity." Jones finally conceded.

"Thank you, Mr. Jones." Lin Mei rose from her seat.

Professor Kaisin followed her out, scowling.

Now she just had to figure out how to convince him to give her the space she needed to fulfill her plan to save Ming. The handsome professor was determined to keep her safe.

And in the days since her rescue from her attacker, she'd had plenty of time to come to terms with the situation, and no longer feared every sound and shadow.

She'd recovered from her traumatic endurance. At least enough to take as much control of her situation as possible.

Jones was right. They were all confined to the ship. No one was going anywhere in between ports... except maybe overboard.

CHAPTER EIGHTEEN

Joe followed Ms. Lau back to their—his—room.

As soon as he clicked the door shut behind himself, he launched into his objections.

"Ms. Lau, I must protest against this line of action. You are far safer here, where I can protect you from another incident."

"Professor Kaisin, Joe, you have been kind and gentlemanly and I have no complaint to offer. However, we cannot endure many more days like this, let alone weeks or months, even!"

Joe removed his glasses with his left hand and rubbed his eyes with his right. She had no idea what kind of people he dealt with in his line of work. "I agree it will be difficult, but I assure you, I've endured far more complicated situations than this. These people—,"

"That man failed to kill me, or throw me overboard," Lin Mei growled, turning toward him. "I survived, thanks to you. And as Mr. Jones said, another attack isn't likely to serve any purpose. I'd rather get on with my life."

"And return to your family?"

Her jaw tightened. "No. Not yet. I still want to assure Ming's safety. What they have planned for her needs to be stopped."

"Lin Mei, there are no laws to protect animals from the will of humans."

"Well, there ought to be!" She stepped forward, index finger raised in his direction. "It isn't right that wealthy aristocrats can do whatever they want to whomever they want."

"What are you going to do?" Joe laughed, "Abscond with the cub and trek your way across South Asia, through the mountains and jungles, to find an ambush of tigers to release her to and hope they don't eat you for your efforts?"

His heart skidded at the ferocity in her eyes.

Her lovely skin darkened with a deep red hue.

Hell's balls, she was thinking of doing exactly that!

"Don't laugh at me." Her eyes glittered.

The notion was preposterous.

"Lin Mei..." The words came out as a strangled plea as Joe struggled against all of the reactions his body churned through. He stared at her. Desperation to make her see just how preposterous the idea was, warred with the desire to drag her into his arms to show her just how much he adored her for it all at once.

She straightened, gaze flicking over his face, from his eyes to his lips.

The tip of her tongue appeared and disappeared before she bit her bottom lip.

His pulse leapt.

Oh no.

She was changing tactic.

Hell's balls.

She was changing tactic and Joe knew it would work on him when it never had before.

It would work because he'd had several long days and nights to understand just how much of a weakness she was to him.

Joe had served the crown for his entire adult life. He knew all the tricks of manipulation—hell, he'd used them numerous times.

He stood still, back to the door.

Leave, Joe.

Give her space to collect herself.

It's cabin fever. Too long confined.

Too much tension between them.

She feels it too.

Dangerous, Joe.

She stepped toward him, face tilted up, voice soft and low. "The way you said my name…"

"A slip."

"Say it again," she breathed, stepping closer. The sound of her voice and the look in her eyes triggered the locked-away fantasies that had occupied his nights since she took up residence in his room.

Joe's fingers itched to unbraid her black hair to revel in the silky strands. He hadn't decided if he wanted to see it fanned out on the pillow around her head as he made love to her or falling in a curtain around him as she straddled him.

Unable to stop himself—unable to deny her, Joe leaned over Lin Mei, teeth gritted, as her name rose in a growl from the root of his desire. "Lin Mei."

Her breath hitched as her eyes locked on his.

They remained staring at one another, each on their own ledge, chests rising and falling in indecision.

Lɪɴ Mᴇɪ's ᴇʏᴇs ꜰɪxᴇᴅ on Joseph's lovely lips. The sound of her name, full of need, sent thrills throughout her body, settling deep at the base of her belly.

She'd meant to scare him into giving up his quest to maintain her safety, but somehow, she'd lost control under the weight of her rising desire for him.

Too many days and nights sleeping in his bed while he slept in a chair just inches away. Too many times, she'd had the thought to just lay aside the duvet and crawl onto his lap and kiss those sweet lips until he opened his beautiful blue eyes.

She desperately wanted him to desire her back. He was so... gentlemanly. Rigid and detached, despite his determination to do right by her.

For her brother.

But now and then, she thought she'd caught lingering glances in her direction.

And an intensity that took her breath away. The way he drew her to him without a single touch.

Had she imagined it?

Now that she pressed him in an effort to get her way, she knew.

I haven't imagined it at all.

The knowledge swept through her.

He'd slipped, crumbling his image of propriety.

Unable to resist, she slid a step closer.

He spoke, but the words delayed reaching her ears over the sound of her racing heart. She blinked.

"I can't protect you if we're apart."

"You already rescued me and made me feel safe. You don't need to protect me anymore," she whispered.

"I want to." His head lowered toward hers.

She rose on the tip of her toes to meet him.

His lips touched hers. Gentle, warm, soft.

Liquid fire curled down through her body, igniting her ardor.

So much better than I dreamed.

She drew a breath against his lips.

He deepened the kiss.

Lin Mei's skin tightened over her entire body, sensing his barely restrained passion just below the surface of his gentlemanly exterior.

His satiny tongue slid along her bottom lip.

She gasped at the sensation. Breathing his name, she met him again, and drew him in, deeper yet.

Bent around her, his lips demanding, drawing her full attention.

Her voice of reason grew faint as they consumed one another.

His warm hands slid around her waist, eliciting shivers.

She pressed herself to his chest to quell them.

He was warm and firm and evoked safety.

Her fingers splayed against the fabric of his jacket, inching up the starched collar to the thick hair curling around his ears.

Her palm slid over his strong jaw, holding him in place as she sank into the sensation of his mouth on hers.

His lips trailed along her own jawline and trailed down the side of her throat.

Every part of her body flared to life as he breathed her name. His hands grasped her bottom, dragging her up against him intimately. His desire for her enflamed her further.

Her head reeled, her fingers trembled, and her voice shook. "Joe."

Disappointment crashed through her when he released her, returning a hand to her waist. The other trailed back up her shoulder and throat to her face.

His gloved fingers touched her cheek as she'd touched his. His mouth reclaimed hers.

Lin Mei craved the intimacy of his touch.

Desperate to feel his naked flesh on her face, she pulled the glove from his hand without breaking the kiss.

The glove fell to the floor.

With reason long gone, she gave in to the haze of need.

Pressing her body to his, she reveled in the sensation of his desire pressed to her lower belly, wanting more.

But she wasn't so lost that the little voice in the back of her head warning her against taking more, went ignored completely.

Not yet.

Not yet, she agreed.

It's just a kiss...

...a kiss to convince him why she needed a room of her own.

Though part of her began to question that plan.

She contented herself with the feel of his lips on hers, her body pressed to his and his hands on her face.

She endeavored to remove the second glove, determined to expose as much of him as she dared, so soon.

Her fingers slid over his left hand, pulling it up to her face, then slipped the glove from his hand, freeing him.

"No!" He gasped, ripping his hand away.

But it was too late.

The empty glove dropped from her fingertips.

Her gaze slid from the metal hand to his eyes.

Shame flickered in the beautiful blue depths before he shuttered it and stepped back.

Her heart tore apart.

"Joseph?" She blinked as she struggled to comprehend what she saw.

Taking another step back, he dropped both hands to his sides.

His suit and hair were disheveled from their intimate contact. His tanned face flushed as his chest rose and fell.

She imagined she looked the same.

Lin Mei's gaze fell to Joe's hands.

He jerked them back, away from her reach.

She swallowed, still reeling from the sudden loss of his body against hers.

He stood rigid, trapped between her and the closed door at his back.

Determined, she grasped both of his hands in hers, holding them up between their bodies so that she may look at them.

He didn't resist her again.

One was his own, strong and warm, with long elegant fingers with clean, trim nails.

The other, a mirror of it, made of a smooth metal. Instead of warm flesh, there was a delicate filigree covering the complex inner workings.

Her hands were small beneath his while she inspected both of his limbs as the shock wore off. Her fingers curled around the edges of both of his hands, her thumbs stroking his knuckles.

"Does it hurt?"

He made to tug from her grasp again, but she held fast.

"Not any longer."

She looked up into his eyes.

Weary and guarded now.

"Will you tell me about it? Someday?"

His shoulders relaxed, and he sighed. "Perhaps."

Bending, she placed a kiss on the back of each hand before releasing them. She moved closer to him while still maintaining minimal space so they were not touching as they had been.

Lifting both her palms to his cheeks, she went up on the balls of her feet to place a third gentle kiss on his lips, eyes closed.

The previous moments had been heated and full of desire.

This last kiss was full of longing and regret.

She released his lips.

He followed her, reluctant to give her up just yet, and pressed his forehead to hers.

Her heartbeat hard in her chest. Desire still raced through her body. It would have been so very easy to give in and finish what she'd started.

"It's too dangerous for us to continue as we were," she whispered, "I must go."

He sighed. "I know."

CHAPTER NINETEEN

THAT SAME EVENING, LIN MEI was granted access to Adelina's room. She immediately got to work inspecting her sister-in-law's performance dresses, desperately needing the distraction.

She divided her worries between Ming and Joe.

Too many times, her thoughts doubled back over the sensation of Joe's lips on hers. The way the heat of his body enveloped her and his expression when she'd removed his gloves.

Once the shock wore off, unasked questions tumbled through her mind in an endless cycle, recounting the moments since they'd met.

As soon as she realized how distracted she was by him, she returned her focus to Ming.

I need to get her out of that cage and back to her family.

She rifled through the dresses again.

Find out who has the key, while earning enough money to get Ming home.

She sighed, studying the selected clothing.

Lin Mei selected one or two to suit her needs, but they would need alteration. Something she was adept at. Living with limited means also meant that clothing needed to be repurposed multiple times.

This room was bigger than the typical guest's room, with extra floor space that she could use to practice the dance, which she hadn't performed since the last festival some months past—with the exception of Joe's visit to her village.

Memories of that day flooded in, causing waves of homesickness to crash over her.

Mama. Her siblings. Their little house tucked between the neighbors'. The village. Her elder brother, whom she knew would move a mountain to ensure her safety.

She drew a shaky breath and closed her eyes.

She opened them and returned her concentration to the task at hand.

After a search of Adelina's room for a mending kit, Lin Mei settled down to work on the dresses.

She didn't have access to any uncut fabric to create a traditional costume, but Adelina did possess one stunning dressing gown made of delicate Chinese silk with a beautiful crane pattern.

Lin Mei just prayed that her alterations wouldn't ruin the garment for Adelina's use afterward.

She would have to alternate between that costume and a European gown for her performances.

Over the few days it took her to make the alterations, she hadn't seen Joe at all, though she would often hear someone stop outside of the door for a moment or two before moving on. After several hours, she set aside the garment she was working on to stretch and rest her eyes from the intense focus on the tiny stitches.

Pacing the room to work out the stiffness, she admired the decor.

Adelina's things lined the walls and filled every corner, but it was all necessary. Costumes and accessories, corsets, crinolines, shoes, face paints and perfumes. There was a shelf dedicated to hair pieces, pins and hats. Everything was ornate, with lace, feathers, and beading.

None of which was evident on Adelina's person when Lin Mei had spent time with her in Hong Kong.

There were two long hair pins set at the forefront of the shelf, beautifully crafted and gleaming and different from everything else.

"A gift from Andrew?" she murmured, sliding a finger over the Chinese pattern engraved along the surface of one.

Lin Mei twisted up her heavy braid, using the hair pins to tuck it into place. A quick assessment in the mirror affixed to the wall confirmed they would be a nice addition to her own costume.

She began the lithe, slow movements of the first dance and on through the next three.

Next, she decided to practice an acrobatic routine, now that her muscles were limber and warm. Ending with a rigorous flip and spin, her braid swung free, striking her face as the pins flew in different directions.

One struck the wall, imbedding itself next to the door, the other bounced along the top of the headboard and clattered behind it.

"*Diel!*" she swore, swiping hair from her face as she stared in horror at the hair pin protruding from the ornate paper adorning the walls.

STANDING BEFORE LIN MEI—Ms. Lau's—door, Joe's hand hovered, prepared to knock.

He'd given this a lot of thought and was determined to follow through.

Sounds of tumbling and thumping were followed by a solid thud right next to the door and footsteps leading up to it.

A strangled "*Diel!*" sounded through the door.

His heart leapt into his throat, triggering his instinct to rush in and rescue her from whatever attack was happening now.

"I told her I couldn't protect her from another room!" he growled, throwing the door open.

Lin Mei leapt backward from the door, crashing into a table as he rushed in.

Joe scanned the room in an instant, heart pounding, ready for violence.

"Professor?"

"Are you alright?" he scanned the space again, but she was clearly alone in the room.

"You frightened the heavens out of me!" she accused, grunting as she attempted to extract an object from the wall.

"What on earth were you doing in here, Ms. Lau? It sounded as though you were being attacked again."

"It's more like I'm doing the attacking," she strained.

He closed the door. "Is that a hatpin?"

"Hair pin." She tugged again, only to have her hands slide off. "Bother!" She huffed, swiping at loose strands of hair clinging to her flushed face.

"Here," Joe strode forward, gave it a sharp tug, then handed it back to her. "How on earth did you manage that?"

"I was practicing." She turned to set it on a nearby shelf cluttered with all manner of hair decorations. "Where are you?" she murmured, standing in the center of the room, hands on hips, scanning the myriad surfaces till she reached the headboard. "Ah yes, back there!"

"Practicing what, dare I ask? And where is who?"

"Dancing." She moved toward the bed, leaning over it. Her exploration continued.

Bottom up, soft gasps escaped as she kneeled on the bed, one hand searching behind the headboard.

Joe cleared his throat, attempting to dispel visions of other bed-appropriate activities suddenly bombarding his brain. "Let me help."

"No, I feel something. I think I've got it... I can feel the tip, but something is blocking my grasp. I just need to give it a tug."

Unable to be of service, Joe stood by as he struggled to control the initial surge of adrenaline to defend her. It pounded through him, converting the blood rush from danger to desire as he watched and waited. And recalled the last time he'd been alone with her.

He kept his distance.

"Ha!" she exclaimed, freeing the second pin and waved it in victory. "Would you place this with the other, please?"

"Of course," he accepted it from her grasp, glad for the distraction.

She slid her hand behind the headboard again and extracted another object as he turned to place the hairpin with its mate.

In the seconds he'd had his back turned, she'd extracted the second object and unrolled and laid out flat on the mattress before her. "What in the heavens are all of these?"

Joe froze.

She freed a coin-sized device from its place behind a leather string securing it. Then her fingers picked out a gleaming set of brass knuckles from their place next to several razor-sharp throwing knives.

Joe's mind raced with what to tell Lin Mei as she peered closer at the brass knuckles, rubbing at some rust-colored residue.

Lies wouldn't form as he watched her process her discovery.

Normally, something quick and reasonable would fly from his lips, redirecting his target with charm or some other fluid explanation.

She turned to him, "This has dried blood on it. I'm sure of it. And these," she held up several identical devices. "I've seen similar ones at the science exposition, only much, much larger. They're communication devices. Hidden in Adelina's room."

Lin Mei blinked once, twice, then shot to her feet. "I have to warn Andrew his new wife is a spy! Those gang members thought I was Adelina when they abducted me! What does she want with Andrew and my family? None of this makes sense..."

As she paced, brass knuckles gripped in her hand, Joseph reeled, not having expected Lin Mei to make the connections so bloody fast.

He should have denied it. He should have offered other explanations as to why such objects would be in Adelina Curren's possessions. Feign shock and total ignorance and not give away his cover as a professor.

Tell her.

The urge to tell her the truth left him reeling.

He shook his head as he studied her, working to untangle what this tool kit represented in alignment with her recent experiences.

My god, she would make a formidable agent.

She'd defended herself against a much larger assailant.

She was dedicated to helping an animal from nefarious experiments.

Fearless.

Determined, intelligent and silent on her feet, he realized as she paced soundlessly.

"They thought *I* was spying on them for the crown or for the constabulary. That means that Adelina probably works for one of them." She glanced at Joe. "Does Andrew know? He *must* know." She resumed pacing and talking to herself. "Not the constabulary. She hasn't been in Hong Kong for long periods. The crown then! Yes! That woman had said there were rumors of a crown agent aboard the ship. But what would the crown want to know about what the gang members in Hong Kong were doing from an airship..."

And on she went, while Joe remained motionless, next to the door, warring with himself over what to say, if anything at all.

"Oh! What was it you wanted, Joe? You came here for a reason?"

"Ah yes, ehm." He drew a deep breath. "I meant to ask you if you would join me for dinner. In the main dining hall."

"Oh," she stared at him, eyes wide.

"Since you're determined to ignore my recommendation that you remain in the safety of your room, I thought it would be beneficial for you to get a sense of what it's like before you perform."

"I see." She seemed to deflate. "Of course, that is a logical approach. How much time do I have to alter another of Adelina's dresses for dinner?"

Joe checked his pocket watch. "A few hours yet."

"I think I can tack something together, but I'd have to be careful not to pull any of the tacking, otherwise the unraveling of my dress may embarrass you." She gave an awkward laugh, cheeks flushing.

"Then I shan't ask you to do acrobatics in the dining hall, as entertaining as that would be," he winked, though that mental image tumbled through his thoughts. He cleared his throat. "I will return at ten to the hour to escort you to dinner."

When she smiled at him, her face glowed and her eyes shone.

Like she had back in her village, before all of this nonsense had tainted her vitality.

Joe recognized the distinct fluttering sensation in his abdomen that he hadn't experienced since he was a youth.

Not even when he'd proposed to Eleanora.

His gaze lingered on her flushed face and messy hair.

You are so beautiful.

Images of their kiss slammed through him, twisting up his insides.

He left before he reached for her.

CHAPTER TWENTY

Lin Mei flew into a frenzied panic.

Another dress to alter—and in such a short amount of time!

She spun, searching for which of Adelina's dresses would be appropriate for her first dinner aboard the Soaring Dragon.

Her heart tripped.

Her first formal, public dinner aboard *the* Soaring Dragon!

With Professor Kai—Joe.

Joe.

Her heart pounded in her chest at the thought of dining in public with him. Without Andrew this time. And without crowding around a small table so that their knees pressed against one another.

That memory inevitably led to more. Those blissful moments of their kiss. Heat rushed through her body.

The reaction to her discovery of his prosthetic limb.

She sighed, glancing at the ceiling.

Please, don't let me mess this up!

Dropping onto the bed, the items that lay strewn across the duvet clinked together, drawing her attention.

Her fingers ghosted over the mystery of the strange kit.

Funny, Joe never said a word about these things.

He hadn't expressed curiosity, nor had he offered any alternate suggestions. No denial as to what they were or that they could have belonged to someone else.

She picked up the small device, twisting a tiny knob with her fingertips. Then she looked at the other items. Several exceedingly sharp knives and what appeared to be a garter with loops.

"To hold the knives? Lock picks? What's in this vial?"

There were hooks and rope and numerous other objects she couldn't guess their function. At least not yet. The thrill of excitement and a secret life set her imagination ablaze.

Lin Mei quickly re-rolled the kit, tied it as it had been when she found it and set it aside to focus on the dress.

"Dress now, spy kit later."

Spy kit. My new sister-in-law is a spy!

But as she worked on the new, unexpected project, her attention returned again and again to the black canvas roll.

And Joe's lack of a reaction to it.

None at all.

No shock or curiosity. No repulsion or intrigue.

Does he know, too?

Would Andrew have told him his wife was a spy for the crown?

She thought back over their time together—in Hong Kong and aboard the ship as she worked on the new dress, which she quickly discovered had hidden pockets built into it.

How many of the other outfits had such alterations?

She set it aside and moved toward Adelina's collection.

Not many.

But there was one 'special' corset of note. It was far more reinforced than the others, though it looked identical. There were hidden metal loops that were also reinforced with enough stitching to support a woman's body weight. It was utterly unbendable, solid like the armor plating that soldiers wore in the old tales.

For the hooks and rope?

Dear heavens, what did Adelina get up to?

Images of Adelina crawling along the outside of the airship like a monkey invaded her thoughts, making her laugh.

"Surely not!" She replaced everything as she'd found it and returned to her task at hand and the suspicious lack of reaction on Joe's part.

The devices.

Had Mr. Kaisin, Joe's father, made them for Adelina? He was a renowned inventor, after all.

What about the weapons? Those hadn't phased him in the least.

He must know something.

Perhaps he'd seen similar equipment among Mr. Kaisin's inventory?

What does Andrew know?

Knowing how stubborn Andrew is, I'll bet he had some strong opinions on the subject, which created problems in their relationship.

Which they must have overcome if they're marrying and starting a family...

And on and on her thoughts tumbled, selecting and discarding, careful to not let her imagination run away with her.

But then, she'd spent days living with a mythical white tiger cub that changed into a little girl that healed her wounds.

Her imagination was leading the charge nowadays.

JOE STRAIGHTENED HIS CRAVAT, vest, and coat.

He checked his watch again. Five more minutes before he went to escort Lin Mei to dinner.

Peering into the small mirror, he ensured his hair was properly coifed. He removed his glasses with their plain glass lenses and polished them until they gleamed.

He stared at them, resting in his gloved hands, tempted to leave them all on the table.

Shed the layers. Let her see who you really are.

Ridiculous.

Glasses back on his face, he checked for any missed patches while shaving. Finding none, he turned away, then spun back again for one last inspection of his teeth.

Good.

Dear god, I haven't been this agitated over dinner in well over a decade.

Not since his time at school with Andrew when they were forced to attend dinners and balls with young ladies from the local etiquette schools.

Those experiences quickly knocked the nerves right out of him as he learned to endure the endless rigid rules both sides were expected to follow. A cumbersome, inelegant dance around anything meaningful.

The height of propriety.

Those long evenings were a vital foundation to the work he did now. Move in and out of society and their predictable protocols.

In fact, it likely fueled his love for the life of spy-craft, moving beneath the surface between the many layers of veneer to what really mattered.

Stale, rigid, reserved.

Oppressed.

Seeking justice and stopping those that also slid along the underlayers to mask their nefarious activities. It took time, and insurmountable patience.

There hadn't yet been any attempts on his cargo, but he attributed that to Lin Mei's presence.

Now that she was no longer inhibiting sneaky activities, he was sure they'd try. Possibly right before they made port at Ceylon. Or right before they reached any of the other ports along the route to London.

He sighed and left his quarters to meet Lin Mei.

Lin Mei.

He smiled.

Everything *society* was not.

Fresh, fluid, fierce.

He'd included her new quarters as part of his daily rounds.

Even days after she'd moved out of his room, the sense of loss persisted.

Joe thought he'd be relieved by the separation, the space to breathe air that wasn't infused with Lin Mei's presence.

Joe stared at her door, wishing it were still his that she lingered behind.

He knocked.

She opened the door, and he lost his breath.

Joe reeled under conflicting layers of emotion ripping through him.

"You are a changeling, Lin Mei," he whispered.

The farm girl was gone, except for the bright eyes staring back at him.

He was thankful that hadn't changed, despite her recent ordeals.

He offered his arm to the graceful woman bound up in satin, lace and beaded refinery. Her simple braid had been tamed into a perfect up-swept knot with careful curls framing her glowing face. His eyes fixed on her full lips, accented with a thin layer of lip rouge.

She accepted his arm. "Do you think I'll fit in?"

"You couldn't possibly, and I hope you never do." He blinked, noting her frown. "What I mean is that, were you less beautiful, you would blend right in."

Her brow cleared, rewarding him with the return of her smile.

She studied his face for a long moment. So long, he was about to ask if he'd missed a spot while shaving after all, when she turned and stepped forward. "Shall we?"

As they approached the entrance to the dining hall, he glanced down at her drawn expression.

"Don't be nervous. You belong here as much as anyone else does."

She nodded, drew in a breath, then eased it out. "It's like the flutters I get before every festival performance."

Butterfly...

"Which are much more important than dinner." He winked, earning another smile.

Be careful Joe. You're the stuffy professor in public.

And as far as Lin Mei is concerned.

He swallowed, suddenly wishing the situation was different. That *he* was different.

Not her brother's oldest friend. Not a crown agent. Not incomplete.

He wanted to let her see who he really was and not who he wasn't.

It doesn't matter what you want, Joe. It matters what she needs—Which is your protection until Andrew can take her home.

If I can even still do that.

Joe's heart did a little flip-flop, then sank as he glanced at her lovely features again.

A member of the dining lounge staff led them past the open stares of the other diners to a table for two, close to the windows which afforded a view of the vast ocean.

He tensed at the proximity of the thin glass barrier.

Through it, the sun cast golden rays, bathing Lin Mei so that she glowed as she settled on her seat.

With his full attention on his companion, he ignored the nothingness beyond the glass. The tension melted away.

The general murmurs of the dining lounge increased in volume.

He also ignored the other diners. He knew them all now, and that they would fixate their curiosity on Lin Mei.

As their server poured wine into their glasses, he observed Lin Mei as her gaze slid around the room, taking in every angle since their approach.

She sipped her wine. Replacing her glass, she clasped her hands in her lap.

Lin Mei smiled as her gaze spanned the room again, hovering on one particular table beyond his shoulder. "Tell me about your journey aboard the ship so far, Professor Kaisin. Who among the guests are the most interesting?"

Joe knew a woman on a mission when he saw one. He suppressed the grin threatening to give away his amusement. He glanced around the room now, noting the positions of the other passengers—many of whom openly stared at Lin Mei. "Who would you like me to begin with?"

Her gaze flicked to the table out of his periphery again, but she said, "How about the couple behind me and go around the room?"

"Newlyweds, very publicly affectionate." He cleared his throat, recalling just how affectionate they were. He'd rounded a corner to find them inappropriately engaged in the corridor outside of their room.

His gaze flicked to the middle-aged couple in the corner. A woman with graying red hair and her Chinese husband held hands across the table. "Friendly couple from Canada visiting his family in Hong Kong while doing the grand tour to celebrate their silver anniversary."

He went on to a larger table. "Dutch Ambassador with his mistress. American railroad baron with his assistant and lover. Both men have wives at home."

She listened with some interest as they waited.

"An Indian prince who was visiting China occupies this next table. He made his way to Hong Kong just for the Soaring Dragon. And a Belgian noble family over there. Several delegates from the middle east. European investors discussing business. A wealthy Argentine family..." and on he went.

"And that table?" she asked, voice low as her gaze rested on her original source of interest. "I saw the blond woman near the ship when I toured it with Andrew. Ming didn't seem to like her."

Joe picked up his near-empty glass, sipped and glanced around to flag the servant to refill it, noting the woman Lin Mei asked about.

"Baroness Von Schlieffen, and her personal assistant, Hermina Engle."

"What is she like?"

"Eccentric. Loud. Typical self-involved rich woman."

Lin Mei nodded, eyes on the woman seated behind Joe.

"Do you think she owns Ming's cage? Or is she a too obvious choice?" she whispered over the edge of her glass.

"I wouldn't be surprised. But if that's the case, then a confrontation with such a woman would be unwise."

Lin Mei's gaze darted back to Joe's face.

"Money, titles, connections, and power."

She nodded. "Like most of the other guests on this ship."

"Precisely." He suppressed the smile that tugged at his lips.

Yes, Lin Mei would make a formidable agent. With a little training...

No. Andrew would flay him for even thinking about nudging his sister toward the agency.

But still...

His gaze drank in the glow of her features as she continued to study the diners, puzzling and assessing.

"Andrew would disapprove."

Lin Mei started at his words, returning her attention to him. "Andrew disapproves of everything." She sipped her drink.

"He just wants to keep his family safe."

"I know." Her brow furrowed. "Too much pressure to succeed when our father was alive and then the pressure to support us after his death."

Joe maintained his silence.

The curtain to the small stage eased open as the first violin strains carried across the room, hushing the murmur of the dining hall.

"I would have loved to see Adelina perform here," Lin Mei said after a few moments.

"She is certainly exceptional. My father speaks highly of her voice."

"Do you think the musicians will know any Chinese music? I should have thought of that before."

Joe assessed the small cluster on the stage, all of varying ethnic backgrounds, including Asian. "Perhaps. We should speak with them after dinner, if you're still determined to do this. You don't have to, you know."

"I will work for my place aboard the ship."

"I would cover the costs," he said.

"No—but thank you."

Moments later, the servers swept through the room carrying heavily laden trays.

For the rest of the evening, Joe enjoyed Lin Mei's company as they dined and enjoyed the music. Their conversation remained light. She asked various questions about the other passengers and their destinations, in between more queries about Joe's early days with her brother.

She eased back into the butterfly he recalled from his time in her village.

His enchantment with her deepened as she stretched her wings.

CHAPTER TWENTY-ONE

AFTER THE DINNER WAS over, Lin Mei approached the musicians to ask after their Chinese repertoire, finding that the violinist knew some traditional music, and even had a mandolin.

A few days later, Jones confirmed the captain's permission to take Adelina's stage. She got to work, meeting and practicing with the musicians.

It surprised Lin Mei to realize that she was excited to perform her traditional dances again.

Her visits with Ming in the cargo hold continued, bringing her extra food and keeping her company. Now that Lin Mei was fully recovered, she even entertained her with dancing.

Sitting next to the cage to catch her breath, she extended a hand into the cage to rub Ming's ears.

The cub's purr was low and lacked enthusiasm. Lin Mei's heart ached for her even as it slowed from the exertion of her dance. "I wish I could just get you out of here and take you back to your family."

She sighed. "This would be so much easier if I could just prove that you were a human."

Ming growled and nipped Lin Mei's hand.

"Ow! I know, I'm sorry. But it would." She pulled her hand away to inspect the minor wound.

Ming whined, sniffing at Lin Mei's hand.

"I know you didn't mean to. It's just a little cut. Don't worry." She offered the cub a smile and pet her with her other hand.

Ming moved forward, nuzzling the hand that she nipped until Lin Mei moved it so that she could see it for herself.

Ming sniffed at the bead of blood, then licked it clean.

Lin Mei watched as the wound, clear of blood, mended itself. "The first time you did that, I thought I'd lost my mind. It's incredible that you can heal others, Ming. You're very special."

And another reason to stay hidden.

"I think I know who has the key to your cage, but all of this sneaking around takes time and I can't do something rash that will get me arrested or taken off the ship."

She sighed, fingers curling through Ming's fur.

"I know Joe—Professor Kaisin—would help us if he knew you were a kidnapped child. But even if I do get the key and unlock your cage, I still have to think of a way to get you off the ship unseen." She turned an assessing eye on Ming. "Do you think you'd fit in a hatbox? No, you wriggle around too much."

Ming groaned.

"I know. I'll figure it out one way or another. And I have to do it before we're both too far away to get back to China."

Lin Mei gave Ming a final ear rub as she rose to leave.

She glanced back at the cub, who stared at her with baleful eyes as she opened the cargo room door. "I promise," she whispered, and left before she gave in to Ming's sad face and went back to her.

Hearing voices, she crept along the corridor, listening. They still hadn't discovered whoever had given the order to get rid of her.

"Mr. Jones is tending to another dispute among the passengers, sir." Lin Mei recognized Mr. Jones' assistant on the security team.

"Thank you."

Lin Mei's heart tripped at the sound of Professor Kaisin's low voice in response, but she held back from making her presence known.

"May I be of assistance?" the man asked.

"I wanted to speak to him about my cargo. I'll return later."

"Sir."

The professor's footsteps retreated away from her. At the creak of the office door, Lin Mei moved forward, careful to ensure Joseph rounded the corner before she approached.

The professor still disapproved of her daily visits, so she opted to go when he was occupied elsewhere.

Jones' assistant glanced up as she moved into the open door. "All quiet with the cub?"

"Yes sir. She is content for now. Same time tomorrow?"

He smiled as he held out his hand. "Good."

She deposited a key on his open palm.

"That cub goes wild when left alone too long, and it seems you're the only one that can calm it."

"What about her owner?"

The man shrugged. "They've been informed of the disturbance it makes. Too busy to care, I suppose." He tucked the key into his vest pocket, lips compressed. "Shame, really. But not my place to insist. And no, Mr. Jones made it very clear we are not to share the owner's identity," he said quickly as she opened her mouth to ask.

She sighed with a little pout.

"Come now, miss. That's the rule, and I know you don't want to get me into trouble," he grinned.

"Don't I?" She grinned back with a wink. "See you in the morning."

"Miss." He bowed politely as she left the office.

She hurried as quietly as possible. When she reached the windowed door to the stairs, she looked in to see if Joseph was still nearby. Noticing his outline in the dark corner of the stairwell, she eased the door open and slipped through the narrow space and closed it.

With his back to her, he stood in the shadows with a woman in his embrace.

Lin Mei gasped.

Both individuals spun toward her as she raced up the steps with a pounding, splitting heart.

JOE FROWNED AT LIN Mei's door as he knocked for the third time.

No sounds were audible beyond the door.

Not here again.

The tiger cub, no doubt.

"How the devil does she manage it?"

He turned, headed toward the staff corridors to talk to Jones.

Jones didn't answer either.

"Mr. Jones is tending another dispute among the passengers, sir."

Joe turned to Jones' security staff member with a nod on his approach. "Thank you."

"May I be of assistance?"

"I wanted to speak to him about my cargo. I'll return later."

"Sir." The man gave him a short bow before entering the security office.

Joe retraced his steps back through the door to the enclosed stairwell. About to mount the steps to the upper level, he paused, hand on the rail. The fine hairs on his arms and back of his neck prickled. "Winter?"

She stepped out of the darkness of the stairwell. "We need to talk."

He leaned to glance up the stairs.

"I haven't heard anyone else. We're alone."

"What do you want?"

"Two things."

Joe glanced back at the door again. Winter clearly didn't want to risk being noticed entering or leaving his room, otherwise she'd have met him there. He hadn't seen her in some time and he'd been preoccupied with his own affairs to prod. "Your case?"

"You should have told me the extent of your injuries, Joe."

Joe's jaw tightened at the words he hadn't expected. "How did you know?"

Winter shrugged.

"It doesn't matter. We both survived." He searched her face.

"We did. Your father?" Her gaze dropped to his left arm.

Joe nodded.

"I want to meet him."

"Why?" his eyes narrowed on his former partner. When it came to his father's cargo, no one was above suspicion, not even Delilah Winter.

"My temporary clockwork needs a permanent replacement, and my physician abandoned me."

"Clockwork?" Joe's brows shot up.

Winter nodded, casting quick glances toward the door as she unbuttoned her blouse.

"Winter—,"

"I wouldn't expose myself if it weren't necessary," she growled.

"Hell's balls, Delilah," he breathed as she pulled the fabric of her blouse aside to give him a full view of the scarred flesh surrounding a metal plate over her heart.

"The shrapnel went deep. Deeper than I could survive long term. They gave me a clockwork to keep me going for now." Her fingers worked over the buttons, securing the blouse.

"For now? It's failing?"

She nodded.

"What of the physician that installed it?"

She blinked and turned her gaze aside, but not before he saw the raw emotion she attempted to conceal. "I can't find him."

Joe lifted a hand to Delilah's shoulder. "I'm sorry," he whispered.

She turned her large, glistening eyes on him before dropping her gaze and reached for his hand. "Me too."

"Old friends, old wounds, eh?"

She lifted his gloved hand. A couple of fat droplets fell down her cheeks.

She's been alone in this.

Joe knew Delilah Winter as well as he knew Andrew Lau. Partners, they'd worked together on and off for years despite their disagreements.

Grudgingly, Joe acknowledged his deep affection for her.

Joe pulled her into his arms to offer some comfort. "Of course, I'll help you. You're not alone." He placed both hands on either side of her face and kissed her forehead.

They were both startled by a soft gasp.

Lin Mei stood inside the closed door, staring at them with wide eyes. Her cheeks flushed as her gaze slid from Delilah's face to Joe's.

The unspoken accusation was clear.

She didn't say a word before running up the steps on silent feet.

"How the bloody hell did she get in here without either of us hearing her?" Delilah growled.

Without another thought, Joe sprinted up the steps two at a time.

Delilah followed.

CHAPTER
TWENTY-TWO

LIN MEI RAN STRAIGHT back through the narrow corridors, heart and thoughts racing.

Shock, betrayal, shame, and heartache surged through her as she rushed into her room, closing and locking the door.

I should have known better.

I was wrong to think that he felt the way that I do.

I should never have initiated that kiss.

Why would Joseph be genuinely interested in me?

Of course, they're not really 'just old friends'.

Her chest heaved as she struggled to regain control of her emotions.

Her fingertips grazed her lips as she recalled their kiss.

The way he'd looked at her...

"Foolish farm girl," she spat at the empty room, fists balled up before her.

She jerked at the knock on her door.

"Lin Mei?" Joe's muffled voice tugged at her heart as it reached through the rising anger. "May we come in?"

We?

The handle jiggled.

Did Ming's cage belong to him, after all?

No. Maybe?

Maybe he'd just been distracting her?

And Ms. Winter? The female accomplice?

"Ms. Lau? This is Delilah Winter. Please let us in so we can talk." Her voice was hushed through the door.

Talk about what?

They both spoke so as not to draw attention to themselves lingering in the hallway.

A fresh wave of anger washed over her.

"Why, so I won't tell my brother?" Her breath shuddered. "So I won't tell him you're both manipulating me not to tell him that you're up to no good, so that he won't have you arrested?"

"Please let us in. It truly isn't what you think." Her voice remained low through the door. "Joe, I have my picks. I can open it."

Lin Mei stepped back from the door. This second statement was even lower than the first, but Lin Mei still deciphered the words.

"No, don't. Let her open it in her own time."

"We don't have much time. This is why I was looking to speak to you in the first place," Ms. Winter said.

"Just give her a moment, Winter." He sighed.

Lin Mei imagined he removed his glasses to rub the bridge of his nose as she'd often observed him do when frustrated or tired.

"Lin Mei, please open the door. You can tell Andrew everything once you're back home."

Still, she hesitated.

Wouldn't a killer say that to gain entrance so they could do away with her without raising the suspicions of security?

She closed her eyes and drew a deep breath to calm herself.

To calm her thoughts.

Before her time confined in the cargo hold, she'd never been so suspicious of people. Cautious, yes. But not paranoid.

It's not unwarranted, Lin Mei. Someone abducted and tried to kill you.

Her gaze fell to Adelina's bundle on her table, then to the hairpins on the shelf.

She drew another breath and armed herself before opening the door.

Relief flooded Joe as the handle clicked and the door swung open.

Lin Mei stood beyond it, expression set. Her eyes glittered with angry determination before turning to Delilah. Lips compressed, she stepped back and allowed them entrance.

Joe moved into the room.

Delilah glanced up and down the hall one last time before she stepped inside and closed the door.

Lin Mei backed up, keeping her distance. Stance rigid, cheeks flushed, her gaze bore into him.

"Lin Mei, it wasn't how it looked. Winter and I are just friends."

Her brow rose, her lips tightened.

Delilah snapped the lock into place, drawing their attention.

"Colleagues. We work together," she said.

"Winter—,"

"Tell her, Joe. She's far more involved than you know. I no longer think there's any point in trying to hide it from her."

"Hide what from me?" Lin Mei demanded.

Joe studied Delilah's face.

How many times since Lin Mei had found Adelina's kit and put most of the puzzle together had he wanted to tell her the truth? Through all of their little conversations over the days since he'd found her in the cargo hold, he'd had to omit factors of his life that he no longer wanted to omit.

Not from her.

It felt wrong keeping things from her or deflecting conversations as they turned too close, and everything began to feel like the lie that it was.

And every time he told her a little lie or omitted something, it was a little slice in his heart.

Lies and omissions that had become natural to him over the years no longer sat comfortably with him. Not when it came to Lin Mei.

"I can see how much she means to you."

His gaze flicked between Lin Mei's taut face and Delilah's soft expression.

Delilah would never encourage him to reveal their secret. *Not without good reason.*

She'd said there were two things she wanted to talk to him about.

The first had been her clockwork.

Whatever the second subject was, it must involve Lin Mei and her case.

"Joe?" Lin Mei's voice drew his attention back to her.

He held her dark gaze for a long moment. "Where is Adelina's kit?"

She stepped aside, revealing the small table behind her, where the black canvas lay unrolled.

Several pieces were missing.

Lifting his gaze from the equipment to her face, her chin tilted upward in defiance.

She'd armed herself before opening the door.

Good.

The corner of his lips quirked.

He couldn't help it.

Joe removed his false glasses as he approached the table, tucking them into his pocket. Placing a finger on each item, he named it and explained its function. Even the gaps, displaying his knowledge of what exactly was in the kit.

When he stepped away again, her eyes were wide, and lips parted.

Her gaze shot from the kit to him, then Delilah and back to him.

He nodded, answering her silent question.

"When you saw us in the stairwell just now, I was asking him for a favor of a... personal nature."

Lin Mei made a little sound of disbelief.

Delilah sighed and unbuttoned her blouse for the second time in less than a quarter hour.

"Ms. Winter, I—," Lin Mei gaped at the sight of Delilah's wounds.

Delilah tapped the metal plate with her fingernail. "I need to speak to his father about mending the clockwork that keeps me alive."

Compassion replaced Lin Mei's shock.

"She sustained that injury when I lost my arm." Joe glanced at Delilah. "We were both seriously wounded during that case. And we haven't really stayed in contact since then. This journey is the first time we've seen each other in a long while."

"Which brings me to our little reunion. The second thing I wanted to discuss with Joe involved you too, Ms. Lau," Delilah said.

Lin Mei slid onto the small bamboo stool next to the table as she stared between the two.

"Andrew? Adelina?"

"Worked with us on many occasions before Andrew left to join the local constabulary—after he and Adelina separated a few years ago," Joe said.

"And he said he wasn't off adventuring," Lin Mei muttered with a scowl. To Delilah she said, "Why do you need me, if you already have connections to them?"

"Aside from the fact that Andrew and Adelina are awaiting the birth of their first child, they aren't the ones that are directly connected to *my* case. You are."

Lin Mei shot to her feet, eyes narrowed on Delilah, a razor-sharp knife in her hand. "I won't let you take Ming away to be experimented on."

"I appreciate your dedication, but I'm determined to protect her, too." Delilah turned to Joe, unconcerned with Lin Mei's weapon. "They're also after something of your father's. I'm not sure what it is. Some kind of adaptor or infuser."

"How can you know any of this?" Lin Mei challenged, knuckles white around the knife handle.

Joe tapped the canvas roll. "Listening devices?"

Delilah nodded. "Joe, Lin Mei has been trying to find a way to get that cub off the ship and back to her family."

"I'm well aware of her intentions."

"You are?" Lin Mei gaped at Joe.

"Because she's a changeling," Delilah said.

Joe blinked at Delilah; his gaze swung to Lin Mei. "They're a myth."

"They're very real. And the Consortium are collecting them."

"What's a consortium?" Lin Mei demanded.

"What the devil for?" Joe scowled, ignoring Lin Mei's question.

"I don't know yet. That's what I have to find out once we get Ming back to her family."

"And figure out which of my father's devices they're after."

"She won't take her human form for anyone but me, and even then it's hard to convince her." Lin Mei's gaze darted between the two as she struggled to process the rapid thread of the conversation.

Delilah said, "she isn't supposed to reveal herself outside of her community at all. She shouldn't have to you, but she is very young and I'm sure she had her own reasons to do so." Turning back to Joe, she said, "Whatever they're doing, Ming isn't the first. I rescued an arctic fox cub a few months ago."

"Your case that led you from Victoria to Hong Kong."

She nodded.

"What does this have to do with the Consortium?"

Delilah drew a deep breath, her fingers drifting over the plate on her chest. She blinked and re-buttoned her shirt, belatedly realizing it still gaped. "After New York happened, Lady Kane visited me during my convalescence. You'd gone home, and no one knew if you were coming back to the agency."

"*I* didn't know if I was going back."

Delilah nodded, her gaze dropping to his hand. "Though I didn't know the severity of your injury, that blast shook us both up pretty bad. Kane knows how dedicated I am." Her eyes caught Joe's. "And that I have no family that needs me, whereas you do. So, once I had time to process that a clockwork heart was keeping me alive, she figured I'd be able to process cases that were... a little more unusual to what we'd previously been exposed to."

Joe rubbed a hand over his face and pinched the bridge of his nose before he turned his full attention to Delilah's face. She wasn't lying. She was a master, but they'd been partnered for too long to not know her tells.

"So not just weapons."

She shook her head. "Not just weapons. Joe, we need you back at the agency. Their activity is escalating at an alarming pace. And they'll be even more motivated to hold on to this tiger cub because she has special abilities, too."

It was Joe's turn to gape.

How much more bizarre could this conversation get?

"Healing," Lin Mei breathed a long sigh. "She can heal people, Joe."

Joe's training took over as he processed what these women were saying. Mythical creature or not, the consortium wanted this cub and Kane, Delilah and Lin Mei all wanted to see it safely returned to its home.

He considered his options.

When it came to the Consortium, there was little choice, especially now that he knew they were indeed, also after his father's work. Again.

How was he going to protect Lin Mei and keep his father's inventory secure all the way to London, while helping Delilah rescue an endangered tiger cub on Kane's orders?

He pinched the bridge of his nose.

"Hell's Balls."

CHAPTER
TWENTY-THREE

WHILE GROWING UP, LIN Mei had heard all the folkloric tales filled with romance, adventure and danger.

They were the pinnacle of any festival. Everyone enjoyed the food, the music and the dances.

But when they were all rolled into one, and performed in the market square, they drew the biggest crowds.

That was how Lin Mei felt now.

Joe. Ming. The spies and the consortium—whatever that was. She still wasn't sure.

Facing the audience spread out from the dining lounge stage, she was deep in the midst of a retelling as she moved to the familiar music of her home.

The heavy tropical air, crowded room, and stage lights all combined with her nerves to dampen her skin, causing her costume to cling and drag over her body.

Bending into lithe forms of various animals, she interpreted each one as they aided the heroine on her journey to defeat the demons, who were stealing children from their villages.

In between the moments of total focus to ensure the movements were perfect, she scanned the dinner guests.

The light was too low to see clearly as she sought the ornate silver key to Ming's cage.

The moonless sky beyond the windows turned them into a wall of darkened mirrors, reflecting the room back to her. The distorted scene added to her nervousness.

Ms. Winter and Joe sat in opposite corners from each other toward the back of the room, watchful.

The agent had failed to gain access to the cargo inventory to confirm who owned the cage. Lin Mei had refused to risk her visitation privileges by sneaking in and stealing it when she had access. If they took away her privileges to the cargo room, she wouldn't be able to get to Ming—to visit or rescue her.

Reluctantly, Winter gave up trying to press Lin Mei on the subject, and Joe suggested they focus on other tactics.

The one that Lin Mei had already decided on while she worked on her costume.

Observe the guests and steal it from them.

That, she would risk.

She just had to confirm which one held the key to Ming's freedom.

They had until they reached Egypt to prepare. That much, Winter had gleaned from her listening devices.

At Ceylon, Joe received a wired response, forwarded from Andrew, which he refused to share with Lin Mei, citing inappropriate language.

"He will meet us in London after the child is born. And I'm to keep you out of trouble."

Lin Mei had scoffed. "Too late for that."

"Out of *more* trouble," he'd scowled.

Now, looking out over the crowd, she eased her posture into a new pose, continuing the story with her body. A section of the story that told of the quest for the treasure. She flowed down the few steps from the stage to the lounge floor, bringing the story to the diners as the music set the tone behind her.

She meandered past the middle-aged Canadian couple, the middle eastern diplomats, and the eastern princes toward the pinch-faced European aristocrat at the center of the room.

It's her, I know it.

Lin Mei bowed before her, arcing her arms so the fabric would flow, light as air above her.

The woman's blond hair towered precariously on her head.

Lin Mei recalled seeing the blond-haired, expensively dressed woman leaning toward Ming's cage on the wharf, while she'd taken the tour of the ship with Andrew. That moment when she'd looked out of the tall windows to view her beloved Hong Kong from the sky.

Her heart squeezed with homesickness.

She blinked away the distracting emotions, along with the unexpected tears blurring her vision.

Lin Mei scanned the woman's array of jewelry glinting in the low light.

Ms. Winter had observed the baroness with a silver chain on most occasions. Whatever it supported was usually tucked into the front of her corset.

Lin Mei knew in her heart it was the key to Ming's cage.

It has to be.

Her breath hitched and her heart sank as she swirled around the woman, fabric-covered arms flowing

No key, no chain.

Diel!

Disappointment twisted her gut as she glided toward the next table. She caught Joe's eye and gave a slight shake of her head.

He nodded in acknowledgment before sipping his after-dinner tea.

The story was nearly finished. Lin Mei slowly retraced her steps to the stage. From the corner of her eye, she noted an unfamiliar figure entered the dining lounge. A woman approached the baroness. Not a servant, but her dress was much less elaborate than the aristocrats.

Lin Mei spun, arcing her arms again, squinting in the low light as the woman took the chair next to the baroness and handed her a silver object.

In a swirl of silk fabric, she spun her way back round the center of the room, by-passing the baroness again as the woman tucked a silver key into the bodice of her corset.

Lin Mei resisted the urge to seize it from her then and there.

Her eyes locked with the newcomer, whose face blanched with shock.

Lifting a foot, Lin Mei extended it above her head, holding the pose for several heartbeats. Then, she finally made her way back to the stage where she wound the story down, lowering herself into a puddle of silk on the stage.

The diners exploded with applause.

She lifted her head and eased to her feet, muscles aching from the physically demanding performance.

Lin Mei smiled and bowed graciously before exiting the stage, heart pounding in victory as the curtain closed.

She thanked the musicians, chest heaving as her pulse still raced.

"It was a pleasure to play and a privilege to accompany your magnificent performance," the lead string player said with a genuine smile and a bow.

Lin Mei dipped her head, returning the smile before making her way to the tiny change room behind the stage.

She stripped out of the costume to hang it up, washed herself, and then struggled into Adelina's altered clothing, hands fumbling.

That woman seemed to recognize me. Is she the same person who met with the man who tried to throw me overboard?

She stopped trying to drag the fabric over her damp skin and drew a deep, steadying breath.

If she is, and she seems to know who I am, I will have to be careful.

Very careful.

I can't lead her or the baroness to suspect Ms. Winter or Joe.

Finally managing all of the laces and fastenings, Lin Mei stepped out into the narrow corridor to make her way to the leisure lounge.

Perspiration slicked her palms as she forced her fingers into Adelina's evening gloves.

It's just until Egypt. You can do this, Lin Mei.

On reaching the open doors of the lounge, she lifted her head, straightened her shoulders, drew a breath and smiled.

CHAPTER
TWENTY-FOUR

JOE'S BREATH STOPPED AS Lin Mei stepped into the arch of the open doors. His heartbeat faster.

My god, she is beautiful.

Cheeks full of color, chin tilted upward, shoulders back like royalty, she strode into the room, drawing the attention of every occupant.

He'd been listening to the passenger chatter closely, and everyone was thoroughly enchanted with her.

He resisted a smile as his gaze swept the room of mingling passengers and card table denizens.

Andrew would be proud of how his sister had blossomed—once he set aside the fear and rage over her endangerment.

Not unwarranted.

The room's gas lamps cast a golden glow over her skin and made her eyes sparkle.

She made her way around the room, greeting and exchanging pleasantries. It was part of an entertainer's duties.

Joe imagined Adelina had done the same, hence how his father had fallen to her charms, too. His father had recounted a lively game of cards with his former colleague in this very room.

His gaze followed Lin Mei, lingering on the lines of her exposed skin just above the low edge of her bodice.

The elegant curve of her collarbones, her delicate silky shoulders. The straight line of her neck and spine. Fine jet hairs curled at her nape, where he desperately wanted to plant lingering kisses.

He cleared his suddenly dry throat and straightened his posture, redirecting his attention.

It was only moments before his gaze returned to the contour of her cheek and the bow of her full, soft lips. Her dark eyes shimmered under the golden glow of the lounge lights as she spoke with the other passengers, keeping her distance from him.

Security remained in the shadowed corners, vigilant in case of trouble—which never happened in the public sections of the ship. Still, their presence kept everyone safe.

Lin Mei was passing Baroness Von Schlieffen's card table when the woman's ornate cane top shot out to block her path. She looked down at it, then at the baroness and smiled.

Joe moved closer, sipping his port, maintaining his air of boredom, ignoring his aversion to the endless view of nothing outside the glass.

He was close enough to hear their exchange.

"Such an intriguing performance," the blonde aristocrat said, her thick accent weighing her words.

"Thank you." Lin Mei dipped in a slight curtsy. When she made to move on, the walking stick remained firmly across the bell of her skirt. "Madam?"

"Japan?"

"China."

"Yun nan?"

"Hong Kong."

"Ah," she barked. "A Cantonese speaker. I am in need of someone with Mandarin. I have an associate I must negotiate with. Well, I shall be very interested to see what your next performances shall be."

The walking stick jerked away from Lin Mei's skirts.

"Madam," she said politely, and strode on to the next cluster of passengers enjoying their evening cards.

Joe remained where he was, looking in Winter's direction long enough to make eye contact before she disappeared from the room. He maintained his post by the windows closest to the baroness' table.

"She is the same one?" The baroness spoke Austrian to her female companion, Ms. Engle.

Joe pulled his watch from his vest pocket, checking the time and glancing around the room as though he waited for someone. When he caught the second woman looking in his direction, he poured all his charm into a smile and gave her a nod and salute with his glass before sipping from it.

Her pale complexion flushed as she suppressed a return smile and answered her mistress.

"She is."

"Too late to do anything about her now. My Abelard won't be pleased with your failure."

"*Freiin.*" The second woman said, with a bow of her head.

The baroness turned in Joe's direction, observing the woman's line of attention. "He is handsome. Professor Kaisin, is it? You should invite him back to our room," she continued in Austrian with a sigh. "We can use a little distraction until we get home. Abelard won't mind. He's good like that."

Joe turned toward the window before either of them looked in his direction again.

"Yes, *Freiin*," Ms. Engle said.

She'd barely said the words when Joe sensed her next to him.

"Lovely, isn't it?" He nodded toward the shimmering jet expanse of ocean beyond the vast windows. Though, to him, it felt more like an abyss.

"Yes it is, Professor. My mistress wishes to invite you for a...private night cap."

Joe glanced toward the baroness, nodding in her direction. She returned the gesture. The corner of her thin lips lifted in a coy invitation while her fingers tightened on the head of her walking stick.

Hell's balls! I'd hoped I was past these types of missions.

He matched her assessing expression. He spared Lin Mei a quick glance.

She was at the far end of the room, occupied with guests.

Weeks ago, he wouldn't have hesitated to do his job.

Now?

He resisted the urge to spare Lin Mei another glance.

Focus on the mission.

Her mission.

And Winter's.

Saving that changeling meant everything to Lin Mei right now.

Despite his disbelief that the myths were real, Joe would do all that he could to ensure they succeeded in taking possession of that key to free the cub.

He would nick it right out of the baroness' ample bodice if he had to.

Winter had insisted that Kane and the Crown had a vested interest in the cub's safe return to its ambush. And the whole thing was to be kept under a firmly shut and weighted lid.

He sauntered toward the baroness' table where he honored her with a deep bow over her gloved hand, catching sight of the silver chain tucked into her bodice on his way down.

Not yet, my boy. Not yet.

As he straightened, he lifted her hand. "Madam?"

His fingers stroked her palm before he released her. "I don't believe we've officially met, have we?"

"I know who you are, Professor Kaisin. I am not so interested in formalities."

"Indeed. And what exactly are you interested in, madam?"

Her pale blue gaze slid down his frame and dragged its way back up. "Lessons."

"Lessons?" He swallowed the last of his port and set the small glass on the table next to his new predator, returning his attention to the woman with the too large eyes, hooked nose and the too thin lips.

"In antiquities," Ms. Engle supplied.

"Antiquities!" He adjusted his spectacles. "My favorite topic. Yes, of course, how may I be of service?" His smile broadened as he clapped his hands together, rubbing his palms in anticipation.

"I have some... pieces I'd like you to assess for me."

Of course you do.

His glance dipped to her bodice where the chain glimmered under the dim lights.

The baroness' smile widened. "I appreciate your enthusiasm, Professor."

She rose from her chair.

With a smirk, her companion fell in step behind her as she led the way out of the lounge.

Joe didn't dare risk glancing in Lin Mei's direction again.

This is going to be the longest night of my life.
For Crown and Country and all that.
And Lin Mei.

CHAPTER TWENTY-FIVE

————— ◈❈◈ —————

LIN MEI JERKED AWAKE.

She lay propped on her elbow, listening for what had roused her.

She turned the knob on her lamp to cast a little more light in the room.

A thump on her door and a muffled groan. "Lin Mei."

Joe?

Is he injured?

Flinging the blanket aside, she ran to the door, her mind racing with what could be wrong.

He fell into the room face down as she whipped the door open.

Dropping to her knees, she struggled to roll him onto his back.

His face and throat looked splotchy.

"Joe?" She said his name, urging him to speak to her as her hands fluttered over him. Smoothing down the sides of his face, through his hair, over his chest and along the sides of his ribs, seeking the injury that felled him.

The top buttons of his shirt were open. She slipped her fingers behind the fabric, smoothing over the hard planes of his shoulders and chest.

No blood.

He shook.

"Joe?" Her voice rose, frantic as her hands moved faster, unable to find the source. "Did you hit your head?" She returned her attention to his hair.

After a few breaths, she realized he wasn't convulsing. He was laughing.

"Stop tickling me," he slurred.

"*Diel*, Joe!" She punched his shoulder, earning a sharp pain for her efforts. "I thought you were hurt!" she hissed, glancing up at the open door.

"Andrew would disapprove of your unladylike language, Butterfly."

She scrambled over to ensure the corridor was empty before shoving his feet into her room. Closing the door, she rounded on him. "What's wrong with you? It's the middle of the night! Are you drunk?"

He crawled toward her bed, where he collapsed with his back propped against its side.

Glasses askew, he grinned. "I got it, Butterfly."

"What?" She scowled at him.

He fumbled with his vest for an interior breast pocket. After several tries, his hand swept out in a clumsy flourish.

A long silver chain dangled from his fingers. An intricately etched silver key swung like a pendulum, glinting in the low light of her room between them.

Her breath stuck in her chest.

The key!

Ming's key!

"But how—," she surged forward to snatch it from him, but he kept it from her reach.

"Shhhh, I don't kiss and tell." His right index finger pressed over his pursed lips while the key continued to swing from the left.

She blinked.

Kiss...

She scanned the splotches on his face and throat again, leaning closer, finger swiping the marks on his skin. "Is that lip rouge? It looks like there are two different shades, Joe? Three?"

No, not three. Two distinct shades, the third color, was the blooming of love bites. She sat back on her haunches, staring at the gentleman professor, rumpled and grinning at her, eyes shining with pride as he continued to uphold the key.

A pit opened in her gut, stealing her breath away again.

Professor of antiquities. Crown agent. Man of the world.

He'd been intimate with other women tonight. Not just one, but at least two.

She couldn't stifle the sensation of illness that made her heart ache, too.

Her eyes flicked to the key.

The baroness *and* her companion?

Heavens.

She blinked away the tears that sprung with the twisting sensation taking over her entire abdomen.

Joe dropped his hands to his lap. "What is it, Butterfly? I thought you'd be happy?"

Her gaze flicked back to his face.

She'd never seen him look so sad.

Like she felt.

Why?

It was just one kiss. Only one.

We aren't promised.

Her breath hitched.

My heart is.

"I had to work really hard for this." His head dropped as he flicked the key with his thumb. "She was really, really good at 'guess the date'. The woman nearly drank me under the table. It was easier once her friend fell asleep, and I did the—." He hiccupped. "Pouring."

Despite her heartache, Lin Mei struggled against the urge to laugh.

"You look like a disheartened little boy."

His head rose so he could meet her gaze. He scowled.

She did laugh then as she leaned forward to straighten his spectacles.

"I don't need those," he said, gaze on her lips. "They're part of my... part."

She shook her head, rose on her knees, and placed them on the nearby table. She leaned toward the washbasin stand for the washcloth. Dipping it in the water, she swiped the soap cake and twisted back toward Joe to clean his face.

"Smells nice."

"It's Adelina's soap."

He nodded. "Didn't think it was yours. Doesn't smell right for you."

She paused. "What do you mean?"

"You're more sweet grass and mountain air."

She resumed her task, processing what he said. "Just like these shades of rouge don't suit you."

He snorted.

Too bad I can't wash away the love bites.

She couldn't help the images that flooded her mind as she stared at him. Two women, embracing and kissing him with such passion that they marked him.

Jealousy surged through her, drawing her closer to him.

She wanted to mark him as *hers*... but couldn't.

Their thick perfumes mingled with alcohol lingered on his clothing.

"I thought you'd be happy, Butterfly," he said again, reaching for her face.

"You kissed them," she whispered, despite herself.

His head jerked back. "It didn't mean anything. Just kisses, nothing more."

"Kisses mean something to me," she choked over the growing lump in her throat as she voiced the twist in her gut. She moved away from him, to hide the illogical pain ripping through her, but he held fast.

Joe's gloved fingers slipped behind her nape, holding her close. Voice soft, he whispered—a breath. "Butterfly."

Her heart pounded as they stared into one another's eyes.

She knew in that moment, without a doubt, there would never be a farmer or a fisherman in her future.

Mama will be so disappointed.

There could *never* be anyone but Professor Joseph Kaisin.

But, Joe would never be hers either.

He was so drunk. Would he even remember this moment in the morning?

He pulled her to him.

She allowed it, closing her eyes.

His lips grazed hers.

Her breath hitched as so many sensations blazed through her body like a mountaintop wildfire during drought season.

They had the key.

Next, they'd be working to get Ming home.

Then, Lin Mei would return to her family and Joe to his.

On opposite sides of the world.

I'm almost out of time.

She opened her eyes to his bright blue ones.

"My Butterfly," he whispered.

Her heart twisted. "You're drunk, Professor."

"I am."

She crawled onto his lap, straddling his thighs so she could face him properly. "Then you won't remember any of this."

Her fingers drifted up the sides of his face, thumbs lingering over his dimples, then up through his thick, curly hair.

Just one.

Just one final kiss before it's too late.

Her hair fell in a curtain around their faces, blocking out the rest of the world as her lips descended to his.

He opened to her, drawing her further in.

She ignored the sharp pain in her heart and focused on the sensations of his lips, tongue, and warm body beneath her.

It wasn't enough.

"I love you, Joe." She hadn't meant the whisper to escape.

Perhaps he hadn't heard. She didn't dare open her eyes.

His arms encircled her hips, crushing her to him.

His desire pressed to her intimately.

Just a kiss, Lin Mei. Nothing more.

She couldn't help herself as she allowed her desire to meet his.

The silk of her nightdress was merely a veil dividing the heat of their bodies.

He groaned, tightening his grip further.

She gasped as the sensations made her head spiral.

She was ablaze, unable to draw breath to cool her thoughts.

Now or never.

Joe released her lips with a sigh. The circle of his arms eased, giving her the space she no longer wanted.

She opened her eyes to his blue gaze.

The cloud of inebriation had cleared.

His gloved thumb stroked over her parted lips.

"I'll remember everything, Lin Mei. No matter how drunk I am." His gaze flicked over her features. "And this? I'd never forget, anyway."

His hands clasped hers, pulling them up between their heaving chests.

The silver key and chain pooled in her palm, warm from his grasp.

"Devilish timing, isn't it, Butterfly? We'll have to move our plans forward." His finger tapped the key.

"Devilish timing indeed," she murmured, staring at the key.

CHAPTER
TWENTY-SIX

Joe's head was a cask of pulsating, sodden cotton, threatening to throw him off-balance with every step toward the coffee urn in the breakfast room.

Tea wouldn't do this morning.

Coffee—several of them were required to alleviate the pressure behind his dry eyes.

He winced against the amplified murmurs, too focused on the task of pouring the liquid into the cup. Even that seemed obnoxiously loud.

"May I be of service, sir?"

Joe jumped and swore under his breath, sloshing the precious brew as a lounge servant appeared next to him.

"Apologies, sir. Why don't you take the seat in the corner while I fix this up and bring it to you?" He nodded to the darkest corner of the breakfast room.

"I'm grateful." He put the cup down, heading to the corner to wait.

'I love you, Joe.'

He'd wanted to say it back, but couldn't.

Those words had brought him several seconds of soaring bliss before he careened into twisting heartache.

It can't be. Not now.

Could it ever be?

He didn't know the answer.

When he'd gone back to his room, he'd retrieved his stash of whiskey and drained it hoping there were answers at the bottom of the flask.

There weren't.

Winter swept past him, making him jump again. "Good work, Kaisin, they're in an upheaval looking for their lost item— however, it's too damned early, Joe," she hissed. "They're going to have security turning the ship upside down to find it before noon tea. Bloody aristocrats and their tantrums."

In his present state, he couldn't tell if she was pleased or annoyed. He decided not to care and shrugged. He'd care after he'd taken care of his torturous headache. "Opportunity."

Her hazel eyes flicked over his face, lingering on his collar. "Timing," she growled and moved on to settle at the table next to his, facing the windows.

The servant deposited the coffee on the crisp linen in front of him, along with some dry toast and a couple of white tablets.

"I am indebted."

"Sir." The servant gave him a slight bow and departed to tend to the next breakfast guest.

"You'd better not be hung over, Kaisin, especially not after rushing our timeline as you did."

"I won't be if you give me a quarter hour, Winter."

"Brilliant."

"Indeed."

He dropped the tablets onto his tongue and washed them down with the hot brew. He winced through the deafening crunching of the dry toast and attempts to swallow the gritty paste without gagging.

His ultra-sensitive hearing alerted him to the swish of fabric and the breath she drew.

"Not yet," he barked before she could speak.

She chuckled. "I don't feel sorry for you."

"I'm a casualty of your mission, you glacial Canadian wench."

She tsked. "Manners, professor."

"Cork it, Winter."

She allowed him five more minutes.

"They pilfered your room, by the way."

"I'm aware." He sighed, rubbing his eyes beneath his spectacles and pinched the bridge of his nose as the tablets worked to churn the cotton out of his head. "While I was preoccupied with opportunity. Whoever did it was good. Barely a thing out of place. Please tell me you haven't planted devices in my quarters."

"Please, Kaisin, not a location I want to be listening in on. I followed a bloke around the ship. Looks like he came aboard at Mogadishu."

Joe nodded, then groaned.

She cleared her throat. "For transparency's sake, I'm fully aware of your adventures last night insofar as Baroness Von Schlieffen—and Ms. Engle—are concerned. Also, not something I wanted to slag my ears with, but I'm committed." She sipped her tea. "And despite the fun hours of artifact hunting in her room, you're the first person they're going to finger for that missing item."

"That game lost all its fun, last night."

Winter snorted.

There was a time he wouldn't have hesitated to engage as far as he needed to go, reveled in it, even. Not anymore. Not since...

Lin Mei.

He'd been truthful when he told her there'd only been kisses, because that's all he could muster, despite his determination to find the key.

He closed his eyes. "They won't find it."

Winter was quiet for a long moment. "I'll keep my eye on her."

"You'd better."

"It's like *that*, is it?"

Joe didn't answer. He didn't have one to give.

Because it was. Like *that*.

"I hope I'm there when Andrew finds out." She cackled with a little too much glee.

"Mind your business," he snapped, "Besides, you've got a mission to complete."

"I can do that *and* be in London in time for Lau's arrival."

"Go away."

"With pleasure, old friend." She rose from her table. "Oh, and they've also been through the cargo for your father's property. They don't appear to have found what they're looking for, as nothing was taken."

Confirmation.

"They won't. It's secure."

Winter's shoulders eased. "Good. I'm going to play shadow. Take care of yourself."

"Thank you."

She nodded and left.

The serving staff cleared away her breakfast remains, then his.

He lounged a little while longer, the room being abnormally quiet with few passengers to observe.

When he reached the exit, Jones was already waiting for him.

"Good morning, sir. Would you care to accompany me to my office?"

Fortified, Joe said, "Lead on."

CHAPTER TWENTY-SEVEN

Lin Mei stared at the silver key in her palm.

It was beautifully made, to match the ornate lock adorning Ming's cage.

There was no question it was the right one.

For weeks, she'd wanted nothing more than to find it.

To free Ming.

And now, the time had come.

Joe had placed it in her palm.

She drew a deep breath as she dropped it into the pocket tied around her waist, hidden under her clothing. The same one she used to hide her mother's rice wine earnings from pickpockets on the wharf.

She surveyed the objects strewn across the length of her bed.

Adelina's black canvas roll. The reinforced corset. Several sets of clothing she'd made for herself and for Ming—if she could convince her to transform. And a pack to carry her in when she wouldn't. There was also a small store of stock-piled biscuits and anything else she could squirrel away that wouldn't spoil.

She didn't wear Adelina's cotton bloomers under the western skirts, but her own linen trousers. There had been a pair of sturdy boots tucked away at the bottom of Adelina's armoire.

The corset required the most time to figure out how it fit and adjust with all its lacings. It wasn't made for Lin Mei's body, but she didn't care about that.

She tucked the pocket into her trousers, securing it behind the waistband before stepping into the layers of petticoats which conveniently hid everything. But inconveniently hindered her movement and weighed her down.

The innermost petticoat had pockets of its own that she used to hide as much of her inventory as she could without creating unsightly and suspicious bulk.

Finally, she pulled on the European style dress with its draped layers and ruffles. Pretty, but cumbersome and impractical—except for hiding things, which it appeared Adelina made the most use of.

Anything she couldn't hide on her person, she would have to hide elsewhere—most likely in the cargo room where she thought she and Ming would make their escape from.

Her fingers grazed over the pocket again.

They'd agreed not to steal it until the night before they were to dock in Egypt.

What was Joe thinking?

Her heart thumped a little harder at the reminder of what would happen next—and of last night's encounter which resulted in heart-melting kisses and the new absolute knowledge her life would never be the same.

Even when she went home.

If she made it back to her family.

Her heart slowed, and she swallowed.

I might not make it home.

This wasn't the first time these thoughts had invaded her consciousness. She'd had plenty of opportunity to philosophize about her fate since her abduction in Hong Kong.

Lin Mei sank to her knees and pressed her forehead to the floor, hands outstretched before her, palms down. "Ancestors. Please, I beg you to help me get little Ming to her family. Even if I can't get to mine."

She repeated her prayer and added requests to ensure the safety and wellbeing of her mother, Andrew and Adelina, and their baby, her siblings, and Joe and Ms. Winter.

Finally, she rose from her impromptu prayers, secured the rest of her equipment, and made her way down to the lower level for her morning visit with Ming.

"Good morning Mr. Jones."

"Ms. Lau," he nodded, stifling a yawn as he rose to fetch her the cargo room key, checking his pocket watch at the same time. "Early for you, isn't it?"

"I'll need to practice the new performance for tonight, so I thought I'd come now."

"I saw last night's show, and it was wonderful!" He beamed at her.

She smiled as she accepted the key. "Thank you, Mr. Jones. I'm glad you enjoyed it." She turned to go as one of his men arrived, breathless and wide-eyed.

"Sir, it's the baroness."

Jones sighed. "Again?"

"Aye, sir."

"I should be back before you're through, Ms. Lau." He closed and locked his office and set off straight away. To his man, he asked, "did she say what it was this time?"

"No sir, just rampaging about another lost, invaluable item."

"Every day, they misplace something and they're all invaluable," he growled as they rounded the corner and disappeared.

Lin Mei hurried to the cargo room, slipped inside and locked herself in.

Ming sat in her cage, ears trained toward Lin Mei. Her front paws did a little tap dance at the sight of her.

"Good morning, Ming." Lin Mei greeted the cub, reaching her hands into the cage to pet her head and rub her ears till she purred. "I have news, little one. We have the key now."

Ming left Lin Mei's embrace to sit at the cage door.

"Oh, not yet. I don't know how to get you off the ship just yet. But soon, I promise."

Ming groaned and dropped in a huff, chin on paws, staring at Lin Mei with forlorn eyes.

"I'm sorry Ming. We have to be patient for just a little longer. And careful. This is our only chance, so we mustn't be discovered."

Lin Mei stood, searching the room, thinking of how best to hide her equipment. "I don't think walking out with the rest of the passengers while you're hidden in a sac will work. You'd squirm so much it would draw suspicion."

She sighed, inspecting the crates in case any had loose lids she could slip things into. Frowning, she ran her fingers over the scrape marks. "It looks as though someone's been forcing these open. That isn't good." She turned to Ming. "If there are thieves aboard looking to steal things in here, they may find our escape equipment."

Lin Mei tried to move some of the crates, thinking to slip her belongings down in behind instead.

The scrape of metal on metal drew Lin Mei's attention to the ceiling. A head full of curly brown hair appeared.

"Ms. Winter?"

"Quick, hand me your supplies and I'll hide them up here," she extended her hand toward Lin Mei.

"How in heavens did you get up there?" she asked, wasting no time in untying the pocketed petticoat so it could drop to her feet. Next, she wriggled out of the dress to divest the reinforced corset. By the time she'd removed everything, she felt significantly lighter.

"The key, Lin Mei, where is it? The only way to ensure the little one's safety is to hide it."

Lin Mei hesitated, hand resting on her skirts covering the inner pocket.

"I know Joe gave it to you and I won't waste his efforts to get it. I assure you, no one has been up here since the ship left Hong Kong. It will be safer here than anywhere else. Hurry, there isn't much time, Lin Mei. They're on their way."

Those words spurred her to action. Fumbling under her clothes, she untied the pocket and passed it up to Ms. Winter, then pulled her dress back in place. "Promise you won't lose it. It's Ming's only hope to get home."

"I promise," she said, dangling upside down from the ceiling, her expression solemn. "My mission aligns with your desire to see her safe with her people. I promise both of you."

Footsteps followed by a knock on the door alerted them to the arrival of the security staff.

Lin Mei glanced up, but Ms. Winter had already disappeared and replaced the grate. She straightened her clothing, heading toward the door, whispering, "We mustn't look at the ceiling, Ming!"

Ming turned her gaze to the door instead.

"Mr. Jones?" Lin Mei unlocked the cargo door with the borrowed key. "Is something wrong?"

The baroness' companion, Ms. Hermina Engle stood next to him, her features drawn, and her cheeks flushed.

"We've just come to ensure the tiger cub is still safely locked in its cage."

"Of course she is," Lin Mei's gaze slid from the woman to Mr. Jones and the security staff loitering behind them. She moved aside so they could search the cargo hold.

"Why is she in here?" Ms. Engle demanded. "No one has permission to interfere with my mistress' property."

"As head of security, I requested that Ms. Lau visit the animal to keep it tame and quiet. As I've explained to your mistress, it becomes unruly and disruptive. It seems to calm when Ms. Lau sings to it so the rest of us can get on with our work."

It was a slight bending of the truth, but not too much so. Their arrangement benefited everyone all around.

"My mistress will not be pleased that you have allowed this person access without authorization. I shall submit a formal complaint to the captain."

"That is your prerogative, madam. However, the captain is aware that I have reported the situation to your Mistress and explained our staffing concerns since she has neglected to provide proper care for her living cargo."

The woman huffed. "Unacceptable. I demand this... person be barred access to Baroness Von Schlieffen's property."

Mr. Jones' straightened with a scowl. "We have answered every one of your Mistress's complaints. We have a duty to all passengers. Not just Baroness Von Schlieffen. I suggest you, or she, spend more time caring for this animal on a daily basis. Ms.

Lau has been kind enough to volunteer her time to see to its comfort."

"I shall find new hired help at the next port. Our previous hire seems to have disappeared unexpectedly since we departed Hong Kong." She glared at Lin Mei.

Lin Mei lifted a brow at the woman's pointed, but unspoken accusation thrown in her direction.

"Your ability to secure quality employees has nothing to do with the Soaring Dragon or her other passengers." Mr. Jones gestured toward the door. "As you can see, the animal is calm and healthy. Now, if you please, I have other calls to answer."

"I refuse to leave while this person is in proximity to my mistress' property."

Jones visibly suppressed a sigh. With forced patience, he turned to Lin Mei. "Ms. Lau?"

"Of course, Mr. Jones. I do not wish my presence to disrupt the operations of the airship." She leveled her gaze at Ms. Engle.

As soon as Lin Mei approached the door to leave, Ming began growling and spitting and throwing herself at the bars of the cage.

Startled, Ms. Engle turned wide eyes on her. "Calm it," she shouted at Jones. "I hate cats."

Jones gave the woman a scathing look as he passed her to approach Ming's cage, who hissed and growled even louder, baring her teeth.

He stopped several feet away. "It appears my presence aggravates the animal, madam."

Lin Mei slipped back into the room. Ming ceased her misbehaving immediately. She crouched next to the cage, whispering in Mandarin. "Be good now. I'll come back if I'm able to."

Ming sighed and resettled with her chin on her paws, eyes on the baroness' companion.

Lin Mei slid past Ms. Engle to exit again, noting the calculated glare in her eye. "Perhaps if your mistress had hired someone suited to dealing with cats, *I* wouldn't need to be in here?"

She handed the cargo room key to Mr. Jones and returned to her room.

There was still much planning to do.

CHAPTER TWENTY-EIGHT

THEY HADN'T ACTUALLY MADE it to Jones' office before they were accosted by servants summoning Jones to various passenger calls, all in states of urgency for their employers.

"I don't know what's going on today, but it seems the ship is in an uproar. Everyone is missing something and screaming about thieves on board."

"Indeed. My room appears to have been searched," Joe said as he accompanied Jones back toward the guest rooms.

Jones looked horrified. "And the baroness' companion, Ms. Engle, came to me, accusing you of stealing something of hers last night. What the bloody hell is going on here?"

"Cabin fever, perhaps?"

"Perhaps. Do you want to make an official report?"

"About my room? Nothing was taken as far as I can tell. Although I would like to inspect my father's cargo at the earliest opportunity."

"Yes, sir. I need to triage these calls in case there truly is something urgent that needs my attention."

Joe pitied the man, who seemed to be running off his feet from start to finish of his shifts.

He stepped into his room, startled to find it crowded with Lin Mei and Delilah.

"I do feel sorry for Jones, but it was necessary. Especially after you knocked a cog out of our plan, Kaisin." Delilah said, brow raised.

"That's your doing?"

She shrugged. "Had to throw suspicion off of you and Lin Mei as best I could. So I did a little personal effects swapping throughout the ship."

Joe groaned. "I hope you don't get anyone fired."

"I can't worry about that. Right now, we have to reconsider our moves. The baroness is meeting someone in Cairo while the ship takes on supplies. She's planning to take the cub's cage with her."

"So we have to get Ming away before that, but how?"

"I was hoping you'd convince her to take her human form and walk her off the ship." Winter said.

Lin Mei shook her head. "She won't."

"Even if that were an option, there aren't any other children on board. Crew would question where this one suddenly came from."

"I thought we could go out through the cargo bay doors once they open for supplies and new passenger cargo, as they've done at a couple of the other ports," Lin Mei said.

Joe removed his spectacles to rub away the remnants of his headache, trying to force clarity. "There are challenges there, too. There will be security monitoring everything that is hauled between that door and the wharf."

"I propose we sneak out and up." Delilah said.

"What? Up? Onto the back of the ship's envelope? How do you propose to get down? Fly? Besides, Ms. Lau doesn't have grappling training for such stunts."

"I borrowed some parachutes from elsewhere on the ship and have them stashed with Lin Mei's things in the ceiling of the cargo room. You can strap her to yourself, and I'll take the cub."

Lin Mei's eyes widened at the proposition.

Delilah went on. "Lin Mei found Adelina's reinforced corset, so securing her to you won't be a problem. We just have to worry about the timing."

"It's a rather dramatic solution, don't you think?"

"We need to get the cub to safety before the baroness takes her to whomever she's meeting with. They're no longer waiting until they reach Europe, which was the original plan. She's to deliver some documents on behalf of the Consortium along with whatever they're trying to steal from you but haven't found yet."

"They've tried the crates in the hold," Lin Mei said.

"It's not in there. But that confirms my suspicions as to what they're after."

"Which is?" Delilah asked, brow quirked. "Whatever it is, it's important to their plan and are determined to find it."

"I'll handle it. Where are you to meet with Kane on the matter?"

"I've wired her from every port, keeping her apprised of our progress. She's on her way to Cairo and the cub's clan is on their way, too. If all goes smoothly, we'll all be back onboard the ship, headed for London, without anyone the wiser."

Lin Mei was looking at Delilah like she'd lost her mind. Her gaze swung to Joe. "Joe?"

He sighed, nodding. "It's doable—if, and that's a rather large if, everything goes smoothly."

"Which it will." Delilah winked at Lin Mei and pat her thigh. "Don't you worry."

Joe clenched his jaw, suppressing the desire to throttle his old partner.

No need to alarm Lin Mei and complicate things.

"You should finalize whatever you need to do, Winter. I propose we stick to the original plan. The key is hidden. Lin Mei is prepared. I have one or two things left to take care of."

Delilah's expression was skeptical.

"Insofar as the timing is concerned. The ship is expected to dock before dawn. You said we have parachutes? Well then, we'll put them to good use on our approach to the city."

"In the dark?" Lin Mei's voice was strained, her eyes wide.

"In the dark," Joe said.

Delilah grinned at both of them.

"YOU'VE BOTH LOST YOUR minds," Lin Mei yelped, jumping to her feet in the cramped quarters of Joe's room.

"You've no need to worry, Lin Mei. We're both experienced and can handle ourselves."

She turned wide eyes on Ms. Winter. "You've jumped out of a moving airship—in the dark?"

She shrugged. "Not exactly. But we can handle most anything. Can't we, Joe?"

"Generally, yes. But I don't think you're reassuring Ms. Lau, Delilah."

"You're not." Lin Mei wrung her hands, moving three paces one way, then back again. It was one thing to admire the view from the heights of an airship and quite another to consider leaping out of one. In the dark.

Adventure.

You wanted adventure, Lin Mei. Well, you've got it.

She glared at Joe, unable to help feeling a sense of betrayal.

The absolute persona of a handsome stuffy professor, with his head full of antiques and his feet solidly on the ground.

Turns out he's anything but.

A laugh bubbled up.

"It will be fine," Ms. Winter insisted, her smile a little less sure as she studied Lin Mei's nervous pacing. "You just have to trust us."

Another laugh, as she looked between the two agents staring at her.

Agents.

And Andrew is one of them? And Adelina too?

No wonder Andrew insisted I stay at home.

Where no one jumped off of airships. In the dark.

Her gaze dropped to Joe's glove covered hand as she recalled Ms. Winter's chest injuries.

Sometimes things go wrong... that's how life is.

Something her father would say.

He said it before he died, having worked himself into illness trying to ensure there was enough money for Andrew's education and the taxes owed on their family farm.

He'd succeeded. Andrew had a western education and employment. Mama had enough to secure the farm and keep the family fed, with a little bit left over to save for the shop she dreamed of.

"You said Ming's family will be in Cairo?" Lin Mei said to Ms. Winter.

She nodded. "Our superior is arranging it. All we have to do is ensure she is there, too."

Since she'd awakened to find herself locked in the cargo hold with Ming, she'd thought only to figure out how to help this child find her way back to her family.

This was Ms. Winter's mission.

Do they even need me?

Would I hinder their success?

"You don't have to do this, Lin Mei. There's no need." Joe's voice was soft. "Delilah and I can take it from here and be back in time for tea."

"I assumed you wanted in, but Joe's right, there's no need for you to risk yourself." Delilah's enthusiasm tempered into an expression of kindness.

"I want to see this through, but I don't see how I could be of use in such circumstances."

Ms. Winter shrugged. "Ming trusts you more than anyone else right now."

Lin Mei considered this.

This is real.

She also considered how her inexperience could cause them to fail—someone could be hurt or captured.

"You're safer here, Lin Mei. Besides, Andrew would try to thrash me if anyone told him I encouraged you to jump out of an airship. Untrained. In the dark." Joe's lips quirked.

Lin Mei laughed. "Yes, yes he would try. But you're not afraid of my big brother. Not really."

"No, not really."

She sighed, looking from one crown agent to the other. "I want nothing more than to see this through. To see Ming returned to the safety of her family. But I'm not trained, and I won't endanger her or you to appease my conscience."

Delilah sniffed. "And here I thought you were fun, Lin Mei." But her eyes twinkled, taking the sting out of the words.

"I am. That's why I'm going to challenge you to teach me how to do fun things when you get back."

"Well, I can do that," Joe straightened. "I'm much more fun than Winter, anyway."

Both women exchanged glances, laughing.

"What? I'm fun."

"Please, Joe." Delilah said, rising from her seat. "You've been wearing the stuffy professor persona for so long you're actually becoming musty yourself."

Joe scowled at Ms. Winter as she reached for the door handle.

"Challenge accepted, by the way," she said to Lin Mei. "See you in the cargo room before dawn." She nodded to Joe and departed.

"I won't be able to get the key to the cargo room from Mr. Jones at that hour." Lin Mei said to Joe, moving toward the door as well.

"Delilah will get us access, don't worry."

She nodded.

He stood, placing a gloved hand on the door above her head.

She looked up into his face. Her heart tripped as he removed the spectacles and tucked them into his vest pocket, holding her gaze all the while.

She pressed her back to the door as he leaned closer.

The heat of his body radiated toward her, drawing her to him.

She lifted her chin a fraction.

"As soon as your cub is safe, I'll show you just how much fun I can be, Lin Mei."

Her breath hitched as his lips descended toward hers. He stopped a breath from her lips. "Andrew and I are going to have a long chat," he whispered, before his lips touched hers.

She pressed her palms flat against the cool surfaces of the door and wall behind her, to resist the lure of pressing them to the expanse of his chest.

The depth of his kiss curled down through her belly, tugging at her toes.

She shivered as he released her mouth as his breath ghosted along her cheek to her throat. She tilted her head with a soft moan.

"Joe."

He returned his lips to hers, ending with the tiniest nibble and a gentle brush of the tip of his nose across hers.

He pulled away from her, his breath quickened, desire glittering in his eyes. His hand dropped away from the door, giving her space to escape.

She said nothing else as she left.

She didn't think she could find words anyway as she thrummed from his kiss, heart skipping as she made her way back to her room.

CHAPTER TWENTY-NINE

In the corridor's darkness, Joe brushed his hand over the thin box tucked into his breast pocket. The captain hadn't minded the impromptu visit for a drink, and chat and the retrieval of his property. He was too wary to risk leaving it behind, though the captain's personal safe was the best place for it.

In case I don't make it back to the ship.

Though he fully intended to.

Joe wasn't sure when he'd decided that he couldn't leave Lin Mei behind.

Truthfully, he hadn't wanted to when he'd left her in the village. Nor at the tea house with Andrew.

During the first part of the journey, thoughts of her lovely face and bright spirit broke the monotony of worrying over his father's property—until that moment when he'd stopped the gang member from hurting her.

Those first nights after her rescue had been hell. Letting her go to Adelina's room? Almost as hard.

And when his butterfly had mended, and he'd tasted the nectar from her lips, there was no going back.

No matter how much he doubted himself.

She'd said she loved him.

What she didn't know was that he had loved her at first sight.

He wasn't going to leave her behind again. Ever. Not without a damned good reason. He flexed the mechanics of his left hand.

Now, Joe knew that death would be the only reason he wouldn't return to her, and he didn't consider that a viable option.

He'd have that chat with Andrew. Andrew would balk. But, Joe suspected he'd have Adelina in his corner to calm any impending rampages before they began.

He smiled.

Joe gave the cargo room door a light tap.

It slid open, revealing Delilah's pale face in the dark. She closed it behind him with a quick glance to ensure they were alone.

From a hidden corner, she extracted a dimmed oil lamp. Turning the light up several notches, she set it aside so they could prepare.

Joe stood before the caged tiger cub, who stared at him, nose twitching. "You're sure this cub is as important as Kane says it is?"

"Have you ever known Kane to be wrong? Besides, I confirmed it."

He turned to Winter, brow raised.

"I saw her change, just the once. And I will tell you, it was an incredible sight that I'll never forget, Joe."

"How the devil did the Consortium get their hands on it?"

Winter shrugged. "Rescue first, investigate second."

"Right. Well, I supposed we'd best be prepared for anything where the Consortium is concerned."

"Indeed," Delilah agreed as she checked her equipment.

He considered the two packs with arm straps, set beside the cargo bay door.

"I checked them. They're good. And strong enough to support two of you—if she changes her mind." Delilah grinned at him.

"I'll convince her not to," Joe growled as he turned his attention to the cargo crates, seeking the one he wanted.

"Good luck with that, Joe. If she does change her mind, there will be nothing you can say to change it back. What do you have there?" she turned to watch him fish another pack out of one of his father's crates.

"Insurance."

She lifted a brow.

"Just something my father was working on. I helped him test it a few years ago. He hasn't had time to finish it, so it may be a little unstable."

"What the blazes is it?"

The cargo bay door swished open, drawing their attention.

"Lin Mei?" Delilah crept forward to confirm the newcomer's identity.

"I had to say goodbye to Ming."

"Of course, we're almost ready to go."

Lin Mei nodded, moving toward the cage, scanning Delilah's pile of equipment by the door.

Joe pulled his father's invention onto his back, its contents sloshing as he checked the straps. He eyed the parachute, gauging how much one pack would impede the other, if at all.

From the corner of his eye, he noted Lin Mei rooting through the parcels on the floor until she held up a cotton pouch and tied it around her waist. From it, she extracted the ornate silver key. She held it up with a sigh, smiled and approached the tiger cub.

Joe huffed a laugh, seeing the clear excitement as the cub's front paws bounced on the floor.

As soon as the door was open an inch, the animal forced its way out, launching itself at Lin Mei, who caught it with a laugh. She hugged it close, eyes closed, she pressed her forehead between its furry ears.

Hoisting the cub in her arms, she approached Delilah and Joe, speaking Mandarin to it, enunciating their names. "I told her you're my friends and you're going to help her return to her family."

Joe nodded.

Delilah beamed. Voice soft, she asked, "May I touch her?"

Lin Mei spoke to the cub, who leaned toward Winter, sniffing.

Winter extended her fingers so it could scent her before it rubbed its face on them. She grinned as she stroked the cub's fur.

She moved toward Joe. After a moment, he too extended his fingers so the cub could know him.

He couldn't help the smile that tugged at his lips as the cub purred under his attention.

"It never occurred to me that I'd ever pet a legendary white tiger, Winter."

"Perks of the job, Kaisin." Delilah grinned, pulling her parachute on, and checked the straps. She picked up another strapped pack from the floor, approaching Joe. "You have no idea what Kane has in store for us when you decide to come back to work."

Joe checked his pocket watch, then tucked it back into his vest so it wouldn't be lost in the jump. "Best get going, Winter."

Lin Mei stepped forward, the cub in her arms, tears in her eyes.

Joe placed his hands on her shoulders. "It will be safe, and we'll be back before you know it."

"Promise me she makes it back to her family." Lin Mei rubbed her cheek against the animal's fur.

Joe glanced at Winter, who nodded. "We promise."

She held his gaze. "I'm trusting you with her life. She is so very precious."

Her hesitance to hand the animal over was palpable.

Joe waited, patient, though fully aware of the passing time before sunrise and their approach to Cairo.

Lin Mei spoke softly to the cub as she lifted it to fit it into the sac slung across Joe's chest.

The animal squirmed, mewling, struggling harder the more Lin Mei insisted on putting it into the bag.

"Ming," she panted, frustrated at the little claws grasping at her shoulders. She spoke in Mandarin again, her voice more forceful as they struggled in opposition to one another, the cub hissing and growling.

Joe dropped one side of the sac, reaching for the animal's scruff, but his hand slid through the shimmering space before him.

His jaw went slack when fur disappeared to reveal a small child clinging desperately to Lin Mei, crying.

"Hell's balls, Winter. Are you seeing this?"

"Isn't she beautiful?" Winter answered, eyes shining in the low lamplight. "Lin Mei, there's nothing for it. We're running out of time. If she refuses to go without you, you'll just have to come with us."

Lin Mei turned terrified eyes on Joe. "She doesn't want me to leave her. She's so afraid."

The naked child in her arms sobbed, repeating her name, her tiny arms nearly choking her.

Joe blinked away the remnants of his disbelief. They truly were running out of time.

"Let's get you prepared, then. No time to waste," he said, heart in his throat.

Gone was his relief that Lin Mei would stay safely aboard the airship.

Delilah jumped to action, grabbed Adelina's reinforced corset and slipped it around Lin Mei's waist, lacing it up quickly.

"As soon as we have you and Joe secured together, I'll help him get the parachute strapped on."

Lin Mei spoke to the child in a soft reassuring voice, taking the bag from Joe. After another brief exchange, the child resumed her animal form and slipped into the sac, her large blue eyes glued to Lin Mei's face from the opening.

Joe and Delilah raced to secure the bag to her chest, tethering it to the corset's metal grappling loops.

Delilah opened the cargo bay door, peering into the darkness, the wind buffeting her hair and clothes.

"I just have to secure the two of you together now," Winter said, slipping the first clip to one of the free loops, then to Joe's own reinforced vest, leaving a few feet of slack still to be taken in. "Where one of you goes, the other has no choice but to follow." Delilah grinned.

"Which will be straight to your deaths if you don't hand over the cub and the infuser adapter."

They all spun at the sound of a woman's accented voice.

Hermina Engle moved toward them, arm extended with a pistol in hand, aimed at Lin Mei's head.

Joe immediately slipped into the space between the pistol and Lin Mei.

The woman held out her other hand, palm up. The pistol rose to his head instead. "Give it over, professor. I know you retrieved it from the captain's safe." She turned to Delilah. "You're not the only one adept at sneaking around."

"What's your plan here? There are three of us and you only have one shot at a time," Delilah taunted.

"This is what you want?" Joe pulled the box from his vest, tightening the fingers of his mechanical hand around the edges. "I can just crush it. Then what?"

"Then one of your companions is dead. Which is worth more to you, Professor?"

Joe hesitated, looking for signs of a bluff. He countered, "Which is worth more to you?"

"Give me the box and I won't shoot anyone. I'll just be on my way."

"And the cub?" Delilah demanded.

"There are others."

But Joe detected a sliver of uncertainty.

"Joe?" He barely heard Lin Mei's small voice over the wind and the engines as the ship continued trundling toward the city.

"Joe, protect that child at all costs." Delilah said, snatching the box from his hand and disappearing out of the open door.

"Delilah!" He spun in time to see her falling, arms and legs outstretched to ride the air ever downward.

It was enough of a distraction for Engle to run forward and grab the spare pack, spinning and shooting Lin Mei in the back as she followed Delilah out into the desert night.

Everything happened so fast. Joe's heart stopped as Lin Mei screamed, falling backward.

His only thought was to grab hold of the door frame with his mechanical hand and the rope tethering them together with his other hand.

The momentum was too much, and the wood splintered under his grasp. Metal scraped on metal and they were both tumbling through the sky after Delilah and the baroness' companion.

INTENSE PAIN STRUCK LIN Mei's back, stealing her breath away and knocking her off balance. Her arms flailed for purchase on the edge of the door, but her fingers slipped right past it as she fell out into the darkness.

"Lin Mei!" Joe screamed after her.

Her entire body jerked again.

Wood splintered and metal screeched as the weight of her body pulled Joe out of the airship with her.

Oh no!

There was only the roar of the wind as she tumbled, with her stomach reaching up into her throat.

She drew a deep breath against the dull pain in her back. Squeezing her eyes shut, she crushed the pack strapped to her chest—as though she could somehow protect Ming.

As though Ming could have a chance to survive if Lin Mei just wrapped herself around her before they hit the ground.

She began praying to every ancestor she could think of in those seconds.

The world was deafening.

A third impact and she wondered if she'd hit the ground already. She then realized they were still far, far above the ground as Joe's powerful arms encircled her as tight as she held Ming.

"Hang on," he shouted as they continued to tumble.

She did.

Arms and legs gripping whatever part of him they could. He drew the rope that tethered them tight, locking her in place before he grappled with the pack on his back.

She noticed the river was a glittering ribbon of black and sapphire under the slivered moon. She focused on the nearby pyramids.

"Hell's balls!" Joe swore. "Where's the switch?"

He grunted and there was a burst of light. They jerked in midair, careening sideways for a few seconds. Joe's cursing continued as he struggled to control whatever he was doing.

She couldn't see anything but the sometimes sky and the more often ground rushing toward them.

I'm going to die.

She spoke to Ming through the sac and the roar of the world around them, not knowing if she could hear her. "You're going back to your family, Ming."

Because even if she and Joe died, somehow, she knew that Ming wouldn't.

Her ancestors would protect her.

Because they had to.

"Hold on, Lin Mei, we're going to land hard. Really hard." Joe shouted as his hands cradled her head.

CHAPTER THIRTY

If I'm not dead already, I fucking hope I am soon.

Joe groaned, taking stock of which parts of his body didn't hurt. There weren't many.

Lin Mei.

The child.

His eyes snapped open as he struggled to sit up, but just flopped.

"Hold still, Joe," Lin Mei pressed a hand to his shoulder. "Let Ming finish.

Finish?

"Wha—,"

"Shhh."

A sharp pinch—or was that a puncture added to all the other painfully throbbing parts of his body.

Then, a weird, moist rasp over the new pain point.

He lifted his head. "Are you hurt?"

"Not anymore. Hold still," Lin Mei snapped, eyes glittering in the darkness.

Joe blew out a breath as the sensation repeated.

"She shot you."

"Adelina's corset stopped it."

"That's good," he wheezed.

They were sheltered under the shade of several palm trees.

His head dropped to the side, where the mangled remains of his father's blast pack lay crumpled on the sand.

He closed his eyes against the terrifying memory of his helplessness when Lin Mei had tumbled out of the airship. He was sure his heart had stopped beating right then.

Clearly, it started again at some point. Probably when he got control of the contraption that kept them from being killed on impact.

A miracle.

There hadn't even been time for prayers.

"What is she doing?" His throat felt as though he'd swallowed several layers of the desert during their rolling stop.

"Healing you. Now be quiet."

He grunted as Ming walked across his stomach, drawing his attention. She ignored him, sniffing at his right arm, then chomped a section that was sore already.

Joe stared wide-eyed as she licked the flesh where she'd drawn blood.

"I think she's priming me for dinner, Lin Mei."

Lin Mei scowled at him. "She is saving your life. Her magic already repaired a few broken bones while you were sleeping."

"Sleeping? How long?"

"Hours." She spared him a glance as she monitored Ming's progress. "You saved all of us with that... machine." She waved a hand at the wreckage.

"Delilah?"

"I don't know," she said, voice soft. Sad.

"She's too much of a spitfire to let us down," Joe said, trying to lie still.

She nodded, blinking away tears that spiked her lashes. "I don't think we're far from the city."

"There's an agency office in Cairo. We'll take Ming there until her family arrives."

"Rest," Lin Mei ordered.

Joe obeyed, relaxing his body as much as was possible under the tiger's ministrations.

Chomp, lick.

Fatigue tugged him back into darkness.

CHAPTER THIRTY-ONE

———⟡———

LIN MEI HUFFED AND stomped her foot as she argued with Ming, one-sided, in her rough Mandarin.

"We cannot walk into the city with you in this form, Ming. We will draw too much attention and it might even get us into more trouble."

Ming flattened her ears and growled at the human clothing Lin Mei held in her hands.

"Well, the sac is ruined and will no longer hide you, either. There's no choice. Be a good girl." She defaulted to pleading, knowing a losing argument with a child all too well, having younger siblings back home.

"What's wrong with the pack?" Joe asked, finally rousing.

"She shredded it to get out."

"Oh."

Lin Mei had awakened to Ming's special method of healing. Again.

She owed the little one so much.

What did it cost her to expend so much energy?

She'd collapsed into a long, long nap next to Joe, while Lin Mei had kept watch.

Joe inspected his clothing and healed wounds. "Incredible."

They both looked as though they ought to be piles of broken bones and rent flesh—Joe more so since he took the brunt of their landing to protect them.

"Magic." Lin Mei corrected.

"I won't argue that. And it explains why the Consortium took her from her clan."

Lin Mei picked through the remnants of their belongings. The smaller pouch of biscuits had survived until Ming had needed to eat to replenish her energy. There were two and a half left. She handed one to Joe, kept the half for herself and put the remaining one away for Ming later.

She squatted next to the tiger cub, speaking Mandarin. "Ming, we want to reunite you with your family as soon as possible, and these clothes are the safest way to do that. Please cooperate."

Ming's gaze slid to Joe.

"He will protect us. Just like he did when we fell from the sky." She sighed. "You know he will. That's why you fixed him, right?"

Ming blinked at her and huffed.

"Come on, the sooner you get dressed, the sooner you see your family."

Ming's ears twitched. She nuzzled Lin Mei's hand.

"I promise to stay with you."

A moment later, Ming's human form shimmered into view. Lin Mei quickly helped her into the clothing she'd made for her.

Ming stood, smoothing her hands down the fabric, reveling in the sensation of the weave under her fingers as Lin Mei fitted the slippers over her small feet. Her blue eyes lifted to Lin Mei's.

She smiled.

Lin Mei smiled back and reached for her hand.

When they drew up alongside Joe, Ming reached for his hand, too.

"Thank you, Ming."

Lin Mei translated.

Ming's smile widened as they began the journey to the edge of the city and through its chaotic, narrow streets.

Eventually, the Soaring Dragon's envelope and gondola were visibly floating above the city.

"Jones will probably be looking for us," Joe said as they approached the edge of a bazaar. "He'll be frantic to find you, especially."

Lin Mei sighed. "I'll make sure Andrew doesn't terminate his position."

Joe shaded his eyes as he studied the buildings surrounding them. "It's been some time since I was in Cairo, but I believe the office is this way." He pointed left. They'd only taken a few steps when a shrill voice cut through the bazaar's deafening cacophony.

"Stop them! Security, stop those two, they stole my property!"

Lin Mei homed in on the source of the impressive, familiarly accented voice. "The baroness," she hissed.

"Let's go," Joe urged them on as several figures moved toward them, but the narrow streets made evasion difficult. Bodies jostled, making it impossible to hold on to Ming's little hand in the crowds.

"Lin Mei!" she cried out when their fingers slipped apart.

"Ming!" Lin Mei couldn't see the child as adults surged into the spaces, rushing through their day. "Ming!"

"Lin Mei!" Ming called again, allowing her to spot her next to an orange cart, tears streaming down her face.

She rushed forward, scooping her up into her arms. Ming's little arms and legs encircled and gripped her as they had in the cargo hold.

She wouldn't let go again.

Joe grabbed Lin Mei's arm in a similar grip, pulling her in another direction and down an even narrower alley way.

"Who are those men? They weren't aboard the ship," Lin Mei shouted as they rounded another corner.

"Hired thugs," he said, twisting to see over his shoulder as he guided them down another lane. And another, twisting and bending back so that Lin Mei quickly lost her bearings.

"Hell's balls!" Joe snapped as they made a wrong turn and faced an enclosure with a locked door. He banged on it with his fist, then moved back toward the alley's entrance, but stopped short.

Three men crowded the narrow lane, creeping forward. The baroness' blond head was visible beyond their shoulders as she followed.

"Return my property, thieves!"

Lin Mei winced at the shrill voice echoing off the confines of the mud-brick walls around them.

Baroness Von Schlieffen shoved her way forward, pushing her hired men aside. Triumph twisted her thin lips as she sauntered forward, looking down her long nose at Lin Mei behind Joe.

"As you can see, we have no property. Now get out of our way," Lin Mei shouted at the aristocrat.

"Where did you hide it?"

"Hide what?"

"My tiger. My gift from my Abelard." The woman strode forward, the men closing in around them. "What's this? Did you trade it for a child?"

Lin Mei pressed her lips together.

Ming hid her face in the crook of Lin Mei's shoulder.

"Then I will take it until you return what is mine."

"You won't touch her," Lin Mei hissed.

Joe stepped between them, drawing the baroness' attention.

She grinned up at him. "Professor, you're looking a little rough. I see you've lost your spectacles. You'll need a new pair if we're to play another round of 'guess that artifact'."

Lightning fast, she reached for Ming's arm to pull her from Lin Mei's grasp.

Equally as fast, Ming turned her face, growling and bit down on the baroness's hand, making her scream. "That little heathen bit me!" Then she gasped, staring into Ming's eyes, leaning closer despite the threat of being bitten again. "Dear god, it's true."

Still in her child form, Ming growled, baring her teeth, sharp canines extended, daring the baroness to reach for her again.

"That child is my tiger, isn't it? Abelard's surprise! Oh Abelard!" She spun on her heel, barking orders at her hired men. "Apprehend them. All of them!"

As they stepped forward to do her bidding, Joe yanked his heavily scuffed leather gloves off, revealing his metal hand. "I suggest you back off if you don't want broken faces."

The men hesitated, eying the metal fist and the set of his jaw as he faced them.

The baroness reached for Ming again and quickly drew her hands back against her chest as she earned another snap of sharp teeth.

"It's about time you got here, Joe. I've been looking all over the city for you three," Delilah's voice rang out from a low rooftop above their alley. "You got lost, didn't you?"

Lin Mei spared Ms. Winter a glance to see two gleaming pistols aimed at their adversaries.

"I told you he'd turn left instead of right." She called toward the only exit as more figures appeared in the narrow space.

Lin Mei smiled, seeing Mr. Jones approach with several of the Soaring Dragon's security staff.

"Mr. Jones, I demand you detain these thieves and return my property to me."

"Property?" Mr. Jones' gaze flicked from Lin Mei to Ming and landed on Joe. "Surely you don't mean the child?"

"Of course I mean that...thing. It's mine. My Abelard gave it to me."

Mr. Jones approached Lin Mei to look into Ming's face. "Ming? Your parents are here to take you home," he said in Mandarin, surprising both Lin Mei and the child.

Ming lifted her face to his at his words.

He smiled at her.

"This child fits the description of a missing girl. We received a wire when we reached port early this morning." He lifted his hand and signaled toward the mouth of the alley.

A group of men and women approached, glaring at the hired men, who looked at one another, shook their heads and left without another look at the baroness.

She screamed at them to stop. They didn't.

Lin Mei's breath caught as she stared at the newcomers.

"Ming, look who's here for you," she breathed.

Ming searched Lin Mei's face, then looked for her clan.

Lin Mei kissed her forehead. "Thank you for helping me, little one."

The tiny child gripped her in a crushing hug, whispering her name.

Lin Mei sniffed, holding back tears as she released Ming to her parents.

"Jones, you'll take the Baroness Von Schlieffen into custody, yeah?" Delilah said from her perch on the roof.

"Yes, Ma'am."

"How dare you—,"

"I suggest you cork it before we hand you over to an ambush of angry tigers, Baroness." Delilah said.

Joe chuckled. "Choose wisely, Madame."

Lin Mei ignored the aristocrat, instead focusing on Ming's family. The rich fabric of their clothing and ornate gold and jeweled hair decoration and brooches denoted an elite class.

Ming whispered to the woman that held her. She had the same brilliant blue eyes that Ming did. The others all had dark brown, like Lin Mei's.

The woman approached Lin Mei, speaking in Mandarin. "Lin Mei Lau? Ming tells me you kept her safe and promised to help her reunite with her family. We are indebted to you."

"I am indebted to Ming. She saved our lives." Lin Mei nodded to Joe.

"You have our gratitude all the same, agent Lau. I shall speak highly of you to your Superior when we meet."

"Oh, I'm not an agent, like they are. I'm just a farm girl, but it would be wonderful if you spoke on their behalf." She smiled at Joe and Ms. Winter.

The woman studied her for a moment, then smiled. "You are far more than just a farm girl." The regal woman bowed her head to Lin Mei, then turned with her people and left the narrow alleyway with their returned treasure.

Ming waved to Lin Mei as they carried her away.

Lin Mei waved back.

"She's right, Lin Mei."

She turned as Joe stepped next to her. "About what?"

"You're far more than just a farm girl."

"Sir, my men have the baroness secured in a prison wagon. They're taking her in for questioning." Jones said to Joe. To Lin Mei he said, "You should join us, Ms. Lau. Becoming an agent would drive your brother mad, but at least you'd have fun doing it." He winked and took his leave.

"Him, too?"

Joe grinned, leaned in close and whispered next to her ear, "We're everywhere."

"Come on, you two, we have a debriefing to attend." Ms. Winter called from the roof above them.

Joe held out his right hand.

Lin Mei dropped her gaze, ignoring it, and instead reached for the other. "Let's go, I'm thirsty."

CHAPTER THIRTY-TWO

--- ◆◦❈◦◆ ---

LIN MEI STOOD AT the Southampton wharf, watching the sleek golden body of the Soaring Dragon as it floated high above.

Excitement fluttered through her as she waited.

Next to her, Joe slid his warm palm against hers, entwining their fingers. He pulled their hands up so that he could kiss the back of her hand, drawing her attention to his face.

His blue eyes sparkled in the morning light behind his new spectacles.

"Don't worry, Butterfly, they'll be happy to see you."

Her heart skipped a beat. "I don't know, Joe. It's been so long, and I don't know that mother will approve of my choices."

"That you're not marrying a local farmer or fisherman?"

"And that I won't be returning home."

"Will you tell them?"

"Is that appropriate? Andrew never told us that he was an agent."

"I'm sure that was to keep your mother's mind at ease."

She nodded, returning her gaze to the airship. "Do you think Delilah will be back from Cairo on this trip?"

"She wired from there, reporting she got a fresh lead on Ms. Engle. She's still tracking the location of my father's invention."

"I'm sorry we lost it." She placed a hand on his sleeve.

"Better it than Ming." He looked down into her face. "You know, Father was far more upset about the news of what they were going to do to her with his work than the loss of the object itself."

Lin Mei smiled at the mention of Mr. Kaisin. "I adore your father."

"And he adores you. He has a stack of letters from Hong Kong, and he's eagerly awaiting your return to the house so that you can read them to him." He placed his fingertip under her chin, tilting it up so that he could admire her lips. "As am I. It will be lovely to have you home after your months away for training."

She rose on tiptoe to touch her lips to his. "I missed you."

He kissed her again, lips lingering on hers before he said, "Have you given my proposal any thought?"

"Now that training is finished and I can protect you if Andrew tries to thrash you for not taking me back to Hong Kong right away?"

Joe chuckled. "Yes."

"Then, yes. I think it's the best way to avert the chaos of his wrath and appease my mother's marital concerns."

"Is that all?"

"I do have one question."

"Which is?"

"Will they allow us to work together? Or will you still partner with Ms. Winter while I have to go off adventuring with some other handsome secret agent?"

"Handsome?"

"A requirement."

"I see. In that case, I shall have to put in a request so that I can ensure I'm the only handsome secret agent I have to worry about getting into—and out of—trouble with you."

"Promise?"

"I'll do my best."

"What better way to spend the rest of my life than to do it adventuring around the world with you? And annoying my big brother in the process."

"There is that."

"He makes it so easy."

"You'll see him soon enough. Can we not talk about him for a little while?"

"Of course," Lin Mei smiled before she returned her lips to his.

The Soaring Dragon Chronicles will continue with *Delilah Winter*'s story... coming soon!

In the mean time, if you haven't read *Adelina and Andrew*'s story '***Return Flight***', get it free when you sign up for my newsletter at **JodiKendrick.com**.

There are plenty more stories loaded with *Romance, Adventure and Passion* available from:

JodiKendrick.com

NOTE TO THE READER

Dear Reader,

Thank you so much for taking the time to read *Changeling*, the second story of the Soaring Dragon Chronicles! If you enjoyed it, please consider leaving a review on your favourite platform.

For free downloads, to join my newsletter and browse my library for more books, visit **JodiKendrick.com**

-Jodi

About Jodi Kendrick

Jodi Kendrick lives in Eastern Ontario Canada with her *Favourite Person* and chompy furbaby, while their adult children explore the wider world.

As a romance author, she writes in paranormal, fantasy, steampunk & gaslamp subgenres, and sometimes delves into urban fantasy and paranormal women's fiction. Her characters are often quirky, sometimes cranky, but they all woman-up and get the job done while their partners ensure they survive with all their bits and bobs attached.

A history enthusiast and word dabbler most of her life, she enjoys exploring 'beyond-the-everyday' and the 'time-before-now', discovering relationship threads weaving individuals through time and place. She's rarely seen without flashy notebooks and colourful pens.

Follow Jodi on Social Media:

Dragon Island
Dragon Heat

Enchanted Ardor
Wish

EveL Worlds : FUCN'A

Tough Nut
Diamond in the Ruff
Honeyed Nut
Gorilla in the Hiss
FUCN'A Collection One
Pedigree Collection

Finely Aged
Dragon Steel

Global Paranormal
Security Agency

Awakened
Surfacing
Polestar
Aquatic Investigations
Prowler

The Kindred Chronicles

Healer
Mercenary

The Soaring Dragon Chronicles

Return Flight
Changeling